THE DIAMOND BROTHERS IN...

Two of Diamonds

This book has been specially written and published for World Book Day 2013. For further information, visit

www.worldbookday.com

World Book Day in the UK and Ireland is made possible by generous sponsorship from National Book Tokens, participating publishers, authors and booksellers. Booksellers who accept the £1 World Book Day Book Token bear the full cost of redeeming it.

World Book Day, World Book Night and Quick Reads are annual initiatives designed to encourage everyone in the UK and Ireland – whatever your age – to read more and discover the joy of books.

World Book Night is a celebration of books and reading for adults and teens on April 23, which sees book gifting and celebrations in thousands of communities around the country.

www.worldbooknight.org

Quick Reads provides brilliant short new books by best-selling authors to engage adults in reading.

www.quickreads.org.uk

THE DIAMOND BROTHERS IN...

Two of Diamonds

ANTHONY HOROWITZ

WALKER
BOOKS

First published individually as *The French Confection* (2002)
and *I Know What You Did Last Wednesday* (2002) by Walker Books Ltd
87 Vauxhall Walk, London SE11 5HJ

This edition published 2012 as Two of Diamonds

2 4 6 8 10 9 7 5 3 1

The French Confection and *I Know What You
Did Last Wednesday* © 2002 Gameslayer Ltd
Introduction © 2012 Gameslayer Ltd
Cover illustrations © 2012 Tony Ross

The right of Anthony Horowitz to be identified as author of this work
has been asserted by him in accordance with the
Copyright, Designs and Patents Act 1988

This book has been typeset in Sabon

Printed in Great Britain by Clays Ltd, St Ives plc

British Library Cataloguing in Publication Data:
a catalogue record for this book is available from the British Library

ISBN 978-1-4063-4741-8

www.walker.co.uk

CONTENTS

Dear Reader,

I knew it was going to be a bad day the moment the woman walked into my office. For a start, she hadn't opened the door, she'd kicked it in – six inches of best Scandinavian pine reduced to matchwood by a single blow from a crocodile skin boot. Personally, I'd have preferred to meet the crocodile. This woman was built like a sumo wrestler. All that was missing was the bald head and the XXL nappy. She had thick lips, thick ears and a thick neck. If you wanted to strangle her, you'd have to get help. She was wearing a fur coat and whatever animal had died, it hadn't been worth it. I won't say she looked brutal, but next to her a brute would have looked sweet.

"What's with the door?" I demanded. "You may have noticed – it has a handle."

The handle fell off and rolled across the floor.

"OK," I said. "It <u>had</u> a handle. You could have knocked."

"I'm in a hurry, Mr Diamond," she replied. "And I mean business."

"Yeah – well being a detective is a mean business," I said. "So perhaps you're in the right place."

And that's what I am, in case you don't know. I'm a private detective. Tim Diamond is the name on the door – although after the woman had finished with it, "im Dim" was all that was left. I have an office in Camden Town and that's where people come when they're in trouble or have nothing to lose. I share the place with my kid brother, Nick, and all you need to know about him is that he's fourteen and he was never invited. He likes to pretend that he's the brains of the operation, which is a bit rich considering he hasn't even taken his GCSEs. And I'm talking as someone who got an A* in embroidery, so I should know.

Nick and I have had plenty of adventures together and we've come so close to death that the three of us are on first name terms. OK, maybe he's helped me from time to time. But he needs me as much as I need him and I don't need him at all.

Anyway, the woman was still staring at me. On second thoughts, I decided she wasn't bad looking. But then my third thoughts told me that my first thoughts had been right and I should keep well away. Too late. She leant towards me. "My name is Denise Johnstone," she said. "And I'm in trouble."

"What sort of trouble is that, Miss Jamestone?" I asked.

"Johnstone. You should know who I am, Diamond. I work for Walker Books. I'm your publisher."

Walker Books. They were an outfit close to the River Thames ... and getting closer. The building should have been knocked down years ago. They published books for kids who didn't like reading – and if you read any of their books, you'd know why. A few years back, they'd hired a guy called Anthony Horowitz to write books about me. I don't know how much they were paying him but looking at his spelling, his prose style and his grammar, I'd say he should have been paying them.

"So what's the problem?" I asked.

"The problem is that we're not selling any of your books. Last year we printed twenty-five thousand copies of 'The Falcon's Malteser'."

That was my first adventure. It was a great story about a dwarf and a box of Maltesers and a secret cache of diamonds. "How many have you got left?" I asked.

"Twenty-four thousand, nine hundred and eighty-four."

I did a quick calculation. "So you only sold twenty-two copies!"

"Sixteen, you idiot. And we had to halve the price to get rid of them. We did a three for two offer for a whole year at WH Smith."

"Did it work?"

"Not exactly. Three people bought two copies." She sighed. "Let's face it, Mr Diamond. Nobody wants to read about a detective who's so stupid he can't even tie his own shoelaces without an instruction manual."

"I don't know who you're talking about, Miss Brimstone."

"We only sold twelve copies of 'Public Enemy Number Two'. And as for 'South by South East', we gave fifty copies to sick children in Africa but the sick children sent them back!"

"Maybe you should sack the guy who does the covers," I suggested.

"Tony Ross is a genius!" the woman exploded. "He does the covers for Horrid Henry and they sell millions. The author's so rich she never gets up before lunch. She writes three Horrid Henry books and then she goes back to bed again. She has gold-plated shelves at Waterstones. Everyone loves her. But you...?"

"Me?" I quavered.

"Tony Ross only does your books on the condition that he doesn't have to read them." The woman stabbed at me with her finger. I was glad she wasn't holding a knife. "I don't know why we publish them. We've had more luck with the non-illustrated version of Where's Wally!"

I sat back. "OK, Miss Gallstone," I said. "I can see you've got a problem. You can't even give these books away!"

"Yes, we can." For the first time, she smiled – though with teeth like hers I wouldn't have bothered. "That's exactly what we can do, Mr Diamond. That's why I'm here. Have you heard of World Book Day?"

"Is that the day you book to fly round the world?"

"No. It's when the whole world buys a book. It's a fantastic idea! About fourteen million children get a £1 voucher..."

"£1 isn't going to go very far between fourteen million children," I said.

She looked at me as if I'd just been sick. Or she was about to be. "They get a £1 voucher each," she snarled. "They take it to their local bookshop and they get to choose one of eight terrific books."

"That is a good idea," I agreed, although it wouldn't have worked at my local bookshop ... but then they only sold one type of book and it certainly wasn't for kids. "So where do I come in?" Actually, I was thinking "Where do I get out?" – but I didn't tell her that.

"This is what we're going to do," she said. "As it happens, I know someone at World Book Day HQ. And I think I can twist their arm into including one of your books in the package."

I glanced at what was left of the door. Have your arm twisted by this woman and the next time you shook hands with someone they'd have to stand behind you.

"We're going to take two of your old stories – 'The French Confection' and 'I Know What You Did Last Wednesday'. We're going to put them in a new cover. Hopefully, nobody will know they've been around for ages. And we'll finally be rid of them!" She giggled. "Better still, there might even be a few kids out there who actually enjoy them. In which case, they might go out and spend real money on some of your other books."

To be honest, I think she was being unfair. These were two of my favourite adventures. The first one took place in France. You may have guessed from the title. Nick and I went to Paris for the weekend and got involved with a vicious gang of drug dealers. It was a complete nightmare or, as they say in Paris, "a complete nightmare" (everyone speaks English). The second story is the one on the cover. It took place on an island off the coast of Scotland and nearly everyone in that nice little picture got killed. Tony Ross may be a genius but he should have packed more red paint.

"All right, Miss Gravestone," I said. "It seems like a great idea. You finally get to shift some copies. You can pretend you're supporting reading. And the kids don't even have to fork out their own pocket money, which they can save up for computer games and cigarettes. What do you want from me?"

The woman frowned. It only improved her face. "I'm sure we don't need to encourage children to smoke, Mr Diamond," she said. "But you can help by writing the introduction for the book. I want you to write something inspirational. Tell them how important reading is. How it develops the mind and the imagination. I'm certain you can manage that."

I wasn't so sure. Reading is great. But what are you going to do when a lunatic who has just murdered seven people tries to push you off a cliff? Wave a Harry Potter at him? Tell him you're a fan of Maisy mouse? (You'll find out if you read this – I'm assuming, of course, you can read.)

OK. So that's the end of the introduction. Support World Book Day. Read because it's good for you. And remember – I get ten per cent of the price on the cover, so read because, above all, it's good for me.

All the best,

Tim Diamond

THE FRENCH CONFECTION

THE FRENCH
FOR MURDER

Everybody loves Paris. There's an old guy who even wrote a song about it. "I love Paris in the springtime...", that's how it goes. Well, all I can say is, he obviously never went there with my big brother, Tim. I did – and it almost killed me.

It all started with a strawberry yoghurt.

It was a French strawberry yoghurt, of course, and it was all we had in the fridge for breakfast. Tim and I tossed a coin to decide who'd get the first mouthful. Then we tossed the coin to see who'd keep the coin. Tim won both times. So there I was sitting at the breakfast table chewing my nails, which was all I had to chew, when Tim suddenly let out a great gurgle and started waving his spoon in the air like he was trying to swat a fly.

"What is it, Tim?" I asked. "Don't tell me! You've found a strawberry!"

"No, Nick! Look...!"

He was holding up the silver foil that he'd just torn off the yoghurt carton and looking at it, and now I understood. The company that made the yoghurt was having one of those promotions. You've probably seen them on chocolate bars or crisps or Coke cans. These days you can't even open a can of beans without finding out if you've won a car or a holiday in Mexico or a cheque for a thousand pounds. Personally, I'm just grateful if I actually find some beans. Anyway, the yoghurt people were offering a whole range of prizes and there it was, written on the underside of the foil.

Congratulations from Bestlé Fruit Yoghurts! You have just won a weekend for two in Paris! Just telephone the number printed on the carton for further details and ... Bon Voyage!

"I've won, Nick!" Tim gasped. "A weekend for two...!" He stopped and bit his thumb. "Who shall I take?" he muttered.

"Oh thanks a lot, Tim," I said. "It was me who bought the yoghurt."

"But it was my money."

"If it hadn't been for me, you'd have spent it on a choc-ice."

Tim scowled. "But Paris, Nick! It's the most romantic city in Europe. I want to take my girlfriend."

"Tim," I reminded him. "You haven't got a girlfriend."

That was a bit cruel of me. The truth was, Tim hadn't been very lucky in love. His first serious relationship had ended tragically when his girlfriend had tried to murder him. After that he'd replied to one of those advertisements in the lonely hearts column of a newspaper, but he can't have read it properly because the girl had turned out to be a guy who spent the evening chasing him round Paddington station. His last girlfriend had been a fire eater in a local circus. He'd taken her out for a romantic, candlelit dinner but she'd completely spoiled it by eating the candles. Right now he was on his own. He sometimes said he felt like a monk – but without the haircut or the religion.

Anyway, we argued a bit more but finally he picked up the telephone and rang the number on the yoghurt carton. There was no answer.

"That's because you've telephoned the sell-by date," I told him. I turned the carton over. "This is the number here…"

And that was how, three weeks later, we found ourselves standing in the forecourt at Waterloo station. Tim was carrying the tickets. I was carrying the bags. It had been more than a year since we'd been abroad – that had been to Amsterdam on the trail of the mysterious assassin known as Charon – and that time we had gone by ferry. Tim had been completely seasick even before he reached the sea. I was relieved that this time we were going by train, taking the Channel Tunnel, although with Tim, of course, you never knew.

We took the escalator down to the international terminal. Ahead of us, the tunnel was waiting: a thirty-two mile stretch linking England and France, built at a cost of twelve billion pounds.

"You have to admit," Tim said. "It's an engineering marvel."

"That's just what I was thinking," I said.

"Yes. It's a fantastic escalator. And so much faster than going down the stairs..."

We had two seats next to each other right in the middle of one of the carriages. The train was pretty full and soon we were joined by two other passengers opposite us. They were both travelling alone. The first was from Texas – you could tell just from his hat. He was chewing an unlit cigar (this was a non-smoking compartment) and reading a magazine: *International Oil*. The other passenger was a very old lady with white hair and skin so wrinkled I was amazed it managed to stay on. I wasn't sure if she had huge eyes or extremely powerful spectacles but every time she looked at me I thought I was about to be hit by a pair of grey and white golf balls. I looked out of the window. The platform was already empty, sweeping in a graceful curve beneath the great glass canopy. Somewhere a door slammed.

The train left exactly on time at ten minutes past ten. There was no whistle. No announcement. I wouldn't have known we had moved if it hadn't been for the slight shudder – and even that was Tim, not the train. He was obviously excited.

About an hour later there was an announcement on the intercom and we dipped into the tunnel carved out underneath the sea. That was a non-cvent too. A car-park, a sign advertising hamburgers, a white cement wall and suddenly the outside world disappeared to be replaced by rushing blackness. So this was the engineering miracle of the last century? As far as Eurostar was concerned, it was just a hole in the ground.

Tim had been ready with his camera and now he drew back, disappointed. "Is this it?" he demanded.

I looked up from my book. "What were you expecting, Tim?" I asked.

"I thought this train went under water!" Tim sighed. "I wanted to take some pictures of the fish!"

The other passengers had heard this and somehow it broke the silence. The old lady had been knitting what looked like a multicoloured sack but now she looked up. "I love taking the train," she announced, and for the first time I realized that she was French. Her accent was so thick you could have wrapped yourself in it to keep warm.

"It sure is one hell of a thing," the Texan agreed. "London to Paris in three and a half hours. Great for business."

The Texan held up his magazine. "I'm in oil. Jed Mathis is the name."

"Why do you call your oil Jed Mathis?" Tim asked.

"I'm sorry?" Jed looked confused. He turned to the old lady. "Are you visiting your grandchildren in Paris?" he asked.

"Non!" the lady replied.

Tim dug into his pocket and pulled out a French dictionary. While he was looking up the word, she continued in English.

"I have a little cake shop in Paris. Erica Nice. That's my name. Please, you must try some of my almond slices." And before anyone could stop her, she'd pulled out a bag of cakes which she offered to us all.

We were still hurtling through the darkness. Tim put away his dictionary and helped himself. At the same time, a steward approached us, pushing one of those trolleys piled up with sandwiches and coffee. He was a thin, pale man with a drooping moustache and slightly sunken eyes. The name on his badge was Marc Chabrol. I remember thinking even then that he looked nervous. A nervous traveller, I thought. But then, why would a nervous traveller work on a train?

Jed produced a wallet full of dollars and offered to buy us all coffee. A free breakfast and we hadn't even arrived. Things were definitely looking up.

"So what do you do?" Erica Nice asked, turning to Tim.

Tim gave a crooked smile. It was meant to make him look smart but in fact he just looked as though he had toothache. "I'm a private detective," he said.

The steward dropped one of the coffee cups. Fortunately, he hadn't added the water yet. Coffee granules showered over the KitKats.

"A private detective?" Erica trilled. "How very unusual!"

"Are you going to Paris on business?" the Texan asked.

Now of course the answer was "no". We were on holiday. Tim hadn't had any business for several weeks and even then he had only been hired to find a missing dog. In fact he had spent three days at Battersea Dogs' Home where he had been bitten three times – twice by dogs. The trouble was, though, he was never going to admit this. He liked to think of himself as a man of mystery. So now he winked and leaned forward. "Just between you and me," he drawled, "I'm on a case." Yes. A nutcase, I thought. But he went on.

"I've been hired by Interplop."

"You mean Interpol," the Texan said.

"The International Police," Tim agreed. "It's a top-secret case. It's so secret, they don't even know about it at the top. In other words…" He gestured with his almond slice, spraying Jed with crumbs, "…a case for Tim Diamond."

The steward had obviously heard all this. As he put down the first cup of coffee, his hands were shaking so much that the liquid spilled over the table. His face had been pale to begin with. Now it had no colour at all. Even his moustache seemed to have faded.

"Where are you staying in Paris?" the old lady asked.

"It's a hotel called The Fat Greek," Tim said.

"Le Chat Gris," I corrected him. It was French for "grey cat" and this was the name of the hotel where Bestlé Yoghurts had booked us in for three nights.

The name seemed to have an electric effect on the steward. I'd been watching him out of the corner of my eye and actually saw him step backwards, colliding with the trolley. The bottles and cans shook. Two packets of ginger-bread biscuits rocketed onto the floor. The man was terrified. But why?

"Paris is so beautiful in the spring," the old lady said. She'd obviously seen the effect that Tim was having on the steward and perhaps she was trying to change the subject before the poor man had a heart attack. "You must make sure you take a stroll on the Champs Elysées … if you have the time."

"How much do I owe you for the coffee?" the American asked.

"Four euros, monsieur…" The steward reached down and picked up the biscuits. The way he took the money and moved off, he could have been trying to get to Paris ahead of the train. I guessed he wanted to get away from us as fast as he could. And I was right. He didn't even stop to offer anyone else in the carriage a coffee. He simply disappeared. Later, when I went to the loo, I saw the trolley standing on its own in the passageway.

Twenty minutes after we'd entered the tunnel, the train burst out again. There was nothing to show that we'd left one country and entered another. The French cows grazing in the fields looked just the same as the English ones on the other side. An official came past, looking at passports. Erica Nice looked at Tim as if puzzled in some way and went back to her knitting. Jed returned to his magazine. We didn't speak for the rest of the journey.

We arrived at the Gare du Nord about an hour later. As everyone struggled with their luggage, Tim gazed at the name. "When do we arrive in Paris?" he asked.

"Tim, this is Paris," I told him. "The Gare du Nord means north station. There are lots of stations in the city."

"I hope you have a lovely time," Erica Nice said. She had an old carpet-bag. It was big enough to hold a carpet – and maybe that was what she had been knitting. She winked at Tim. "Good luck with the case, mon ami!"

Meanwhile, the Texan had grabbed a leather briefcase. He nodded at us briefly and joined the queue for the exit. Tim and I retrieved our two bags and a few moments later we were standing on the platform, wondering which way to go.

"We'd better find the Metro," I said. Bestlé had given us some spending money for the weekend but I didn't think it would be enough for us to travel everywhere by taxi.

Tim shook his head. "Forget the metro, Nick," he said. "Let's take the tube."

I didn't even bother to argue. I knew a little French – I'd been learning it from a little Frenchman who taught at our school – and I knew, for example, that Metro was the French word for tube train. On the other hand, I didn't know the French for idiot, which was the English word for Tim. I picked up the bags and prepared to follow him when suddenly we found ourselves interrupted.

It was Marc Chabrol. The French steward had reappeared and was standing in front of us, blocking our way. He was terrified. I could see it in his bulging eyes, the sweat on his cheeks, the yellow and black bow tie which had climbed halfway up his neck.

"I have to talk to you, Monsieur," he rasped. He was speaking in English, the words as uncomfortable in his mouth as somebody else's false teeth. "Tonight. At eleven o'clock. There is a café in the sixth *arrondisement*. It is called La Palette…"

"That's very nice of you," Tim said. He seemed to think that Chabrol was inviting us out for a drink.

"Beware of the mad American!" The steward whispered the words as if he were too afraid to speak them aloud. "The mad American…!"

He was about to add something but then his face changed again. He seemed to freeze as if his worst nightmare had just come true. I glanced left and right but if there was someone he had recognized in the crowd, I didn't see them. "*Oh mon Dieu!*" he whispered. He seized Tim's hand and pressed something into the palm. Then he turned and staggered away.

Tim opened his hand. He was holding a small blue envelope with a gold star printed on the side. I recognized it at once. It was a sachet of sugar from the train. "What was all that about?" Tim asked.

I took the sugar and examined it. I thought

he might have written something on it – a telephone number or something. But it was just a little bag of sugar. I slipped it into my back pocket. "I don't know..." I said. And I didn't. Why should the steward have left us with a spoonful of sugar? Why did he want to meet us later that night? What was going on?

"Funny people, the French," Tim said.

Ten minutes later, we were still at the Gare du Nord. The money that Bestlé had given us was in English pounds and pence. We needed euros and that meant queuing up at the Bureau de Change. The queue was a long one and it seemed to be moving at a rate of one euro per hour.

We had just reached the window when we heard the scream.

It was like no sound I had ever heard, thin and high and horribly final. The station was huge and noisy but the scream cut through the crowd like a scalpel. Everybody stopped and turned to see where it had come from. Even Tim heard it. "Oh dear," he said. "It sounds like someone has stepped on a cat."

Tim changed thirty pounds, and taking the money we moved in the direction of the Metro. Already a police car had arrived and several uniformed gendarmes were hurrying towards the trains. I strained to hear what the crowd was saying. They were speaking French, of course. That didn't make it any easier.

"What's happened?"

"It's terrible. Somebody has fallen under a train."

"It was a steward. He was on the train from London. He fell off a platform."

"Is he hurt?"

"He's dead. Crushed by a train."

I heard all of it. I understood some of it. I didn't like any of it. A steward? Off the London train? Somehow I didn't need to ask his name.

"Tim," I asked. "What's the French for murder?"

Tim shrugged. "Why do you want to know?"

"I don't know." I stepped onto the escalator and allowed it to carry me down. "I've just got a feeling it's something we're going to need."

LE CHAT GRIS

Le Chat Gris was in the Latin quarter, a dark, busy area on the south side of the River Seine. Here the streets were full of students and the smell of cheap food. It was a small, narrow building, wedged between an art gallery and a café. A metal cat, more rusty than grey, hung over the main entrance and there were brightly coloured flowers in the front windows. On closer inspection they turned out to be made of plastic.

The reception area was so small that if you went in too quickly you'd be out the other side. There was a receptionist standing behind the desk which was just as well as there wasn't enough room for a chair. He was an old man, at least sixty, with a crumpled face and something terribly wrong with his eyes. When he looked at our passports he had to hold them up beside his ear. He took our names, then sent us to a room on the fifth floor. Fortunately there was a lift but it wasn't much bigger than a telephone box. Tim and I stood shoulder to shoulder with our cases as it creaked and trembled slowly up. Next time, I decided, I'd take the stairs.

The truth was that Bestlé hadn't been too generous with the accommodation. Our room was built into the roof with wooden beams that sloped down at strange angles. It made me think of the Hunchback of Notre Dame. You needed a hunched back to avoid hitting your head on the ceiling. There were two beds, a single window with a view over the other rooftops, a chest of drawers and a bathroom too small to take a bath.

"Which bed do you want?" I asked.

"This one!" Tim threw himself onto the bed next to the window. There was a loud "ping" as several of the springs snapped. I sat down, more carefully, on the other bed. It felt like the duvet wasn't just filled with goose feathers, but they'd also left in half the goose.

We dumped our luggage and went out. This was, after all, Thursday morning and we only had until Sunday afternoon. Back in the reception area, the receptionist was talking to a new arrival. This was a square-shouldered man with narrow eyes and black, slicked-back hair. He was wearing an expensive, charcoal grey suit. Both of them stopped when they saw us. I dropped the key with a clunk.

"*Merci,*" I said.

Neither of the men said anything. Maybe it was my accent.

There was a mirror next to the front door and but for that I wouldn't have noticed what happened next. But as Tim and I made our way out, the man in the grey suit reached out and took my key, turning it round so that he could read the number. He was interested in us. That was for sure. His eyes, empty of emotion, were still scrutinizing us as the door swung shut and we found ourselves in the street.

First the death of the steward on the train. Then the last whispered warning: *"Beware the mad American!"* And now this. There was a nasty smell in the air and already I knew it wasn't just French cheese.

"Which way, Nick?" Tim was waiting for me, holding a camera. He had already taken three photographs of the hotel, a streetlamp and a post-box and he was waiting for me in the morning sunlight. I wondered if he had remembered to put in a film.

I thought for a moment. I was probably being stupid. We were here in Paris for the weekend and nothing was going to happen. I couldn't even be sure that it really was Marc Chabrol who had fallen under the train. "Let's try down there," I said, pointing down the street.

"Good idea," Tim agreed as he turned the other way.

What can I tell you about Paris? I'm no travel writer. I'm not crazy about writing and I can't usually afford to travel. But anyway...

Paris is a big city full of French people. It's a lot prettier than London and for that matter so are the people. They're everywhere: in the street-side cafés, sipping black coffee from thimble-sized cups, strolling along the Seine in their designer sunglasses, snapping at each other on the bridges through eighteen inches of the latest Japanese lens. The streets are narrower than in London and looking at the traffic you get the feeling that war has broken out. There are cars parked everywhere. On the streets and on the pavements. Actually, it's hard to tell which cars are parked and which ones are just stuck in the traffic jams. But the strange thing is that nobody seems to be in a hurry. Life is just a big jumble that moves along at its own pace and if you're in a hurry to leave then maybe you should never have come there in the first place.

That first day, Tim and I did the usual tourist things. We went up the Eiffel Tower. Tim fainted. So we came down again. We went to the cathedral of Notre Dame and I took a picture of Tim and another of a gargoyle. I just hoped that when I got them developed I'd remember which was which. We went up the Champs Elysées and down the Jardin des Tuileries. By lunch-time, my stomach was rumbling. So, more worryingly, were my feet.

We had an early supper at a brasserie over-looking another brasserie. That's another thing about Paris. There are brasseries everywhere. Tim ordered two ham sandwiches, a beer for him and a Coke for me. Then I ordered them again using words the waiter understood. The sandwiches arrived: twenty centimetres of bread, I noticed, but only ten centimetres of ham.

"This is the life, eh, Nick?" Tim sighed as he sipped his beer.

"Yes, Tim," I said. "And this is the bill."

Tim glanced at it and swallowed his beer the wrong way. "Ten euros!" he exclaimed. "That's … that's…!" He frowned. "How much is that?"

"A euro's worth about seven old francs," I explained. "It's about seventy pence. So the bill is about seven quid."

Tim shook his head. "I hate this new money," he said.

"I know," I agreed. "Because you haven't got any."

We were walking back in the direction of the hotel when it happened. We were in one of those quiet, antique streets near the Seine when two men appeared, blocking our way. The first was in his forties, tall and slim, wearing a white linen suit that was so crumpled and dirty, it hung off him like a used paper bag. He was one of the ugliest men I had ever seen. He had green eyes, a small nose and a mouth like a knife wound. None of these were in quite the right place. It was as if his whole face had been drawn by a six-year-old child.

His partner was about twenty years younger with the body of an ape and, if the dull glimmer in his eyes was anything to go by, a brain to match. He was wearing jeans and a leather jacket and smoking a cigarette. I guessed he was a body-builder. He had muscles bulging everywhere and a neck that somehow managed to be wider than his head. His hair was blonde and greasy. He had fat lips and a tiny beard sprouting out of the middle of his chin.

"Good evening," White Suit said in perfect English. His voice came out like a whisper from a punctured balloon. "My name is Bastille. Jacques Bastille. My friend's name is Lavache. I wonder if I might speak with you."

"If you want to know the way, don't ask us!" Tim replied. "We're lost too."

"I'm not lost. Oh, no." Bastille smiled, revealing teeth the colour of French mustard. "No. But I want to know what he told you. I want to know what you know."

Tim turned to me, puzzled.

"What exactly do you mean?" I asked.

"The steward on the train. What did he tell you?" There was a pause. Then ... "Lavache!"

Bastille nodded and his partner produced

35

what looked like a little model of that famous statue, the Venus de Milo. You know the one. The naked woman with no arms that stands somewhere in the Louvre.

"No thank you," Tim began. "We're not..."

Lavache pressed a button and ten centimetres of razor-sharp metal sprang out of the head of the statue. It was a neat trick. I don't think the real statue ever did that.

Tim stared at it.

"Where is it?" Bastille demanded.

"Your friend's holding it in his hand!" Tim gasped.

"Not the knife! *Sacré bleu!* Are all the English such idiots? I am talking about the object. The item that you were given this morning at the Gare du Nord."

"I wasn't given anything!" Tim wailed.

"It's true," I said, even though I knew that it wasn't.

Bastille blinked heavily. "You're lying."

"No, we're not," Tim replied. "Cross my heart and hope to..."

"Tim!" I interrupted.

"Kill them both!" Bastille snapped.

They really did mean to kill us there and then in that quiet Paris street. Lavache lifted the knife, his stubby fingers curving around the base, a bead of saliva glistening at the corner of his mouth. I glanced back, wondering if we could run. But it was hopeless. We'd be cut down before we could take a step.

"The older one first," Bastille commanded.

"That's him!" Tim said, pointing at me.

"Tim!" I exclaimed.

The knife hovered between us.

But then suddenly a party of American tourists turned the corner – about twenty of them, following a guide who was holding an umbrella with a Stars and Stripes attached to the tip. They were jabbering excitedly as they descended on us. There was nothing Bastille and Lavache could do. Suddenly they were surrounded, and realizing this was our only chance I grabbed hold of Tim and moved away, keeping a wall of American tourists between us and our attackers. Only when we'd come to the top of the street where it joined the wide and busy Boulevard St Michel did we break away and run.

But the two killers weren't going to let us get away quite so easily. I glanced back and saw them pushing their way through the crowd. Bastille shoved out a hand and one of the tourists, an elderly woman, shrieked and fell backwards into a fountain. Several of the other tourists stopped and took photographs of her. Bastille stepped into the road. A car swerved to avoid him and crashed into the front of a restaurant. Two lobsters and a plateful of mussels were sent flying. Someone screamed.

It still wasn't dark. The streets were full of people on their way to restaurants, too wrapped up in their own affairs to notice two English visitors running for their lives. I had no idea where I was going and I wasn't going to stop and ask for directions. I grabbed Tim again and steered him up an alleyway with dozens more restaurants on both sides. A waiter in a long white apron, carrying several trays laden with plates and glasses, stepped out in front of me. There was no way I could avoid him. There was a strangled cry, then a crash.

"Excusez-moi!" Tim burbled.

Fortunately, I didn't know enough French to understand the waiter's reply.

The alleyway brought us back to the Seine. I could see Notre Dame in the distance. Only a few hours before we had been standing on one of its towers, enjoying the view. How could our holiday have become a nightmare so quickly?

"This way, Tim!" I shouted.

I pulled him across a busy street, cars screeching to a halt, horns blaring. A gendarme turned round to face us, a whistle clenched between his teeth, his hands scrabbling for his gun. I swear he would have shot us except that we were already on the other side of the road and a few seconds later Bastille had reached him, brutally pushing him out of the way. The unfortunate gendarme spun round and collided with a cyclist. Both of them collapsed in a tangle of rubber and steel. The last I saw of the gendarme, he had got back to his feet and was shouting at us, making a curious, high-pitched noise. Evidently he had swallowed his whistle which had now got lodged in his throat.

The river was now right in front of us with a pedestrian bridge leading over to the other side. Bastille and Lavache were already crossing the road, blocked for a moment by a bus that had slipped in between them and us.

"The river!" I said.

Tim reached into his pocket and took out his camera.

"No!" I yelled. "I don't want you to photograph it! I want us to cross it!"

We ran onto the bridge, but I hadn't taken more than a few steps before I saw that we'd made a bad mistake. The bridge was closed. There was a tall barrier running across the middle of it with a MEN AT WORK sign – but no sign at all of any men actually at work. They had left their tools, though. There was a wheelbarrow, a pile of steel girders, a cement mixer … even if we could have climbed over the fence it would have been hard to get through.

"We've got to go back!" I shouted.

But it was too late. Bastille and Lavache had already arrived at the entrance to the bridge and were moving more slowly, both of them smiling.

They knew they had us trapped. Lavache had his knife out. It was difficult to hear with the noise of the traffic, but I think he was humming.

We couldn't go back. We couldn't climb the fence. If we jumped over the side, we'd probably drown. This was only March and the water would be ice-cold. Just twenty metres separated us from the two Frenchmen. There was nothing we could do.

And that was when I saw the boat. It was what they called a Bateau Mouche, one of those long, elegant boats with glass windows and ceilings that carry tourists up and down the river throughout the day and night. This one was full of people enjoying a dinner and dance. I heard the music drifting up to us. They were playing a waltz, the "Blue Danube". A strange choice considering they were on the Seine. Already the boat was slipping under the bridge. Another few seconds and it would have disappeared down towards the Eiffel Tower.

"Jump, Tim!" I ordered.

"Right, Nick!" Tim jumped up and down on the spot.

"No. I mean – jump off the bridge!"

"What?" Tim looked at me as if I was mad.

Bastille was only five steps away from us now. I ran to the edge of the bridge, hoisted myself up and jumped. Tim did the same, a few seconds behind me. I caught a glimpse of

Bastille, staring at us, his face twisted between anger and amazement. Then I was falling through space with the river, the bridge and the boat corkscrewing around me. I thought I might have mistimed it but then my feet hit something and I crashed onto the deck. I was lucky. I had hit the front of the boat where there was a sheet of tarpaulin stretched out amid a tangle of ropes. It broke my fall.

Tim was less fortunate. He had jumped a few seconds after me, allowing the boat to travel a few metres further forward. I heard the glass shatter as he went feet first through the glass roof. There were more screams and the music stopped. I pulled myself up and gazed groggily through a window. Tim had landed on one of the tables and was lying there, sprawled out, surrounded by broken plates and glasses and with what looked like a whole roast duck in his lap.

"Que fais-tu? Qu'est-ce que se passe?"

A man in a blue uniform had appeared on the deck. He was staring at me in horror. It was the captain of the Bateau Mouche. There were a couple of waiters with him. I didn't even struggle as the three of them grabbed hold of me. I wondered if they were going to lock me up or throw me over the side. Certainly it didn't look as if they were going to invite me in for a dance and something to eat.

I twisted round and took one last look back at the bridge. Bastille and Lavache were leaning over the side, watching, and as I was dragged inside they vanished, swallowed up in the gathering gloom.

DOWN AND OUT

You won't meet many thirteen-year-olds who have been locked up in prisons on both sides of the Channel, but I'm one of them. I did time in Strangeday Hall, sharing a cell with Johnny Powers, England's public enemy number one*, and here I was in prison in Paris, this time with Tim. It was half past nine in the evening. We'd been given dinner – bread and water – but the fact that it was French bread and Perrier didn't make it taste any better.

Miraculously, neither Tim nor I had been hurt jumping from the bridge. The captain had locked us both up in the kitchen on board the ship and by the time we docked, the police were already waiting. I suppose he must have radioed on ahead. I hadn't tried to argue as we were thrown into the back of a van and driven at high speed through the streets of Paris.

* See *Public Enemy Number Two*

Nobody spoke English and even if they had they wouldn't have believed us. I assumed they'd call the British consul or someone. I would leave the explanations until then.

Neither of us had said anything for a while but at last Tim broke the silence. "That's the last time I buy a Bestlé yoghurt," he muttered.

"It wasn't their fault, Tim," I said, although I knew how he felt. We hadn't even been in Paris one day and we'd witnessed one murder, been chased by two killers and were now locked up ourselves. It was probably just as well that we weren't planning to stay a whole week. "I just wish I knew what it was all about," I added.

"They tried to kill us, Nick," Tim explained. "They nearly *did* kill us!"

"I noticed, Tim. But why?"

Tim thought for a moment. "Perhaps they don't like foreigners?" he suggested.

"No. They were looking for something. Something they thought we had." I already knew it had to be tied in with Marc Chabrol, the steward we had met at the Gare du Nord, and the sachet of sugar he had given us. But what could be so important about a packet of sugar? It was still in my back pocket. I reached in and took it out. "This is what they were after," I said.

"Sugar?"

"Unless there's something else inside..."

I was about to open it there and then but at that moment the door opened and a young policeman with close-cropped hair and glasses walked in. I slipped the sachet back into my pocket. I could always examine it later.

"This way, please," the policeman said.

He led us back out and down a corridor, then into an interrogation room that smelled of cigarette smoke. There was a table and three chairs but nothing else, not even a window. A naked light bulb hung on a short flex from the ceiling. The policeman gestured and we all sat down.

"You are English," he said.

"That's right," I said. The man obviously had a first-class brain.

"This is an outrage!" Tim exclaimed. "You can't keep us here. I demand to speak to the British ambassador! If the British ambassador is busy, I'll speak to his wife."

The policeman leaned forward. "First of all, monsieur, I can keep you here for as long as I wish," he said. "And secondly, I doubt very much that the British ambassador would be interested in you. Or his wife!"

"Why wouldn't he be interested in his wife?" Tim asked.

The policeman ignored him. "You and your small brother have caused great damage to one of our Bateaux Mouches," he went on. "It is most fortunate that nobody was injured. I wish to know why the two of you jumped off the bridge. You were trying to commit suicide, perhaps? Or could it have been a joke?"

"It was no joke," I said. "There were two men trying to kill us..."

The policeman looked at me in disbelief.

"It's true," I went on. "They said their names were Bastille and Lavache. They had a knife..."

"Tell me your names," the policeman commanded. He took out a notebook and prepared to write.

"I'm Tim Diamond," Tim said. "You may have heard of me."

"No, monsieur..."

"Well, I'm a well-known detective back in London." Tim pointed at the notebook. "That's the capital of England," he added, helpfully.

The policeman paused and took a deep breath. He was getting older by the minute. "I am aware of that," he said. "May I ask, what is your business here in Paris?"

"Of course you can ask!" Tim said.

The policeman groaned. "What is your business?" he demanded.

"We're on holiday," I told him. "We only arrived today. We're staying in Le Chat Gris in the Latin quarter..."

The policeman looked at me strangely, as if he were seeing me properly for the first time. "Le Chat Gris..." he repeated. He closed the notebook. "Could you please wait here for a minute."

He stood up and left the room.

In fact it was ten minutes before he returned. The moment he walked in, I noticed there was something different about him. He was brisk, emotionless. And when he spoke, he did his best not to meet our eyes. "I have spoken with my superior officer," he said. "And he says that you are free to go!"

"How can we be free to go when we're locked up in here?" Tim asked.

"No, no, no, monsieur. He says that you may leave."

"They're unlocking the door and letting us out," I explained.

"As far as we are concerned, this incident is closed." The policeman did the same to his notebook.

"What about Bastille and Lavache?" I asked.

"We have no record of these men. It is our view that they do not exist!"

"What?"

"You jump off the bridge for a joke or maybe as a game and you make up the story of the killers to explain your actions. That is the view of my Superintendent."

"Well, he can't be as super as all that," I growled.

But there was no point arguing. For whatever

their reasons, the French police had decided to let us go. As far as I was concerned, I just wanted to get out of jail. And out of Paris too, for that matter. I'd only been there for a day but so far our visit had been less fun than a French lesson – and twice as dangerous.

"Let's go, Tim," I said.

And we went.

It was almost eleven o'clock by the time we got back to the Latin quarter, but the night wasn't over yet. Tim wanted to stop for a beer and I was still anxious to open the packet of sugar that was burning a hole in my back pocket. We looked for a café and quite by coincidence found ourselves outside an old-fashioned, artistic sort of place whose name I knew. It was La Palette, the very same café where the train steward, Marc Chabrol, had asked us to meet.

He wasn't there, of course. Right now, if Chabrol was sipping coffee, it was with two wings and a halo. But there was someone there that we recognized. He was sitting out in the front, smoking a cigar, gazing into the night sky. There was no way I'd forget the hat. It was Jed Mathis, the businessman we had met on the train.

Tim saw him. "It's Ned," he said.

"You mean Jed," I said.

"Why don't we join him?"

"Forget it!" I grabbed Tim and we walked

forward, continuing towards our hotel.

"But Nick! He paid for the drinks on the train. Maybe he'd buy me a beer."

"Yes, Tim. But think for a minute. What's he doing at La Palette?" I looked at my watch. It was eleven o'clock exactly. "It could just be a coincidence. But maybe he's waiting for someone. Maybe he's waiting for us! Don't you remember what Marc Chabrol said?"

"He asked us if we wanted to buy a KitKat."

"Yes. But after that. In the station, he warned us about someone who he called 'the mad American'. Jed Mathis is American! He said he was from Texas."

"You think Mathis killed Chabrol?"

"Mathis was on the train. And Chabrol ended up underneath it. I don't know. But I don't think we should hang around and have drinks with him. I think we should go home!"

We hurried on. Le Chat Gris loomed up ahead of us, but before we got there I noticed something else.

There was a man standing opposite the hotel. It was hard to recognize him because he was holding a camera up to his face, taking a picture. I heard the click of the button and the whir as the film wound on automatically. He wasn't a tourist. That much was certain. Not unless his idea of a holiday snap was two English tourists about to check out. Because the photograph he had taken had been of us. There could be no doubt about it. I could feel the telephoto lens halfway up my nose.

He lowered the camera and now I recognized the man. He had been standing in the reception area that morning when we left: a dark-haired man in a grey suit.

Marc Chabrol, the steward.

Bastille and Lavache.

And now this.

Just what was happening in Paris and why did it all have to happen to us?

A car suddenly drew up, a blue Citroën. The man with the camera got in and a moment later they were roaring past us. I just caught a glimpse of the driver, smoking a cigarette with one hand, steering with the other. Then they were gone.

Tim had already walked into the hotel. Feeling increasingly uneasy, I followed him in.

We took the key from the squinting receptionist and took the stairs back to the top of the hotel. There were a lot of them and the stairway was so narrow that the walls brushed both my shoulders as I climbed. Finally we got to the last floor. Tim stopped for breath. Then he unlocked our door.

Our room had been torn apart. The sheets had been pulled off the bed and the mattress slashed open, springs and enough hair to cover a horse tumbling out onto the floor. Every drawer had been opened, upturned and smashed. The carpet had been pulled up and the curtains down. Tim's jackets and trousers had been scattered all over the room. And I mean scattered. We found one arm on a window-sill, one leg in the shower, a single pocket under what was left of the bed. Our suitcases had been cut open and turned inside out. We'd need another suitcase just to carry the old ones down to the bin.

Tim gazed at the destruction. "I can't say I think too much of room service, Nick," he said.

"This isn't room service, Tim!" I exploded. "The room's been searched!"

"What do you think they were looking for?"

"This!" I took out the packet of sugar. Once again I was tempted to open it – but this wasn't the right time. "This is the only thing Chabrol gave us back at the station. It must be the object that Bastille was talking about." I slid it back into my pocket, then thought again. It seemed that Bastille was determined to get his hands on the sugar. I wouldn't be safe carrying it. It was better to leave it in the hotel room. After all, they'd already searched the place once. It was unlikely they'd think of coming back.

I looked around, then slid the sugar into the toilet-roll in the bathroom, inside the cardboard tube. Nobody would notice it there and the police could pick it up later. Because that was the next step.

"We've got to call the police," I said.

"We've just come from the police," Tim reminded me.

"I know. But if they see our room, they've got to believe us. And as soon as they're here, I'll show them the packet. Maybe they'll be able to work the whole thing out."

I looked for the telephone and eventually found it – or what was left of it. You'd have to be an expert at electronics or at least very good at jigsaws to use it again.

"Why don't we talk to the man downstairs?" Tim asked.

I thought of the squinting receptionist. Only that morning he'd been talking to the man in the grey suit, the one who'd just taken our photograph.

"I don't trust him," I said. At that moment I wouldn't have trusted my own mother.

Tim held up a short-sleeved shirt. It had been a long-sleeved shirt when he had packed it. He looked as if he was going to burst into tears. At least he could use the rest of the shirt as a handkerchief if he did.

"Let's go back down, Tim," I said. "We can call the police from the lobby. I noticed a phone booth."

"What's the French for 999?" Tim asked.

"17," I replied. I'd seen it written next to the phone.

But the phone in the hotel was out of order. There was a sign on the window reading *"Hors de service"*. I translated for Tim and he went over to the receptionist. "We want to call the police," he said.

"Please?" The receptionist narrowed his eye. I think he would have liked to have narrowed both his eyes, but the one on the left wasn't working.

"No," Tim explained. "Police." He saluted and bent his knees, doing an imitation of a policeman. The receptionist stared at him as if he had gone mad.

"Les flics," I said.

"Ah!" The receptionist nodded. Then he leant forward and pointed. "You go out the door. You turn left. Then you take the first turning left again," he growled. He actually spoke pretty good English even if the words had trouble getting past his throat. "There's a police station just at the next corner."

We left the hotel, turned left and then immediately left again. We found ourselves in a narrow alleyway that twisted its way through the shadows before coming to a brick wall.

"This is wrong," I said.

"You don't want to go to the police anymore?" Tim asked.

"No, Tim. I still want to go to the police but this is the wrong way. It's a dead-end."

"Maybe we have to climb over the wall."

"I don't think so..."

I was getting worried. After everything that had happened to us so far, the last place I wanted to be was a dead-end ... or anywhere else with the word "dead" in it. And I was right. There was a sudden squeal as a van appeared racing towards us. The squeal, incidentally, came from Tim. The van was reversing. For a moment I thought it was going to crush us, but it stopped, just centimetres away. The back doors flew open. Two men got out.

Everything was happening too quickly. I couldn't even tell who the men were or if I had seen them before. I saw one of them lash out and Tim spun round, crumpling to the ground. Then it was my turn. Something hard hit me on the back of the head. My legs buckled. I fell forward and one of the men must have caught me as I felt myself being half-pushed, half-carried into the back of the van.

Tim was next to me. "Some holiday!" he said.

Then either they hit me again or they hit him. Or maybe they hit both of us. Either way, I was out cold.

PARIS BY NIGHT

I knew I was in trouble before I even opened my eyes. For a start, I was sitting up. If everything that had happened up until now had been a horrible dream – which it should have been – I would be lying in my nice warm bed in Camden with the kettle whistling in the kitchen and maybe Tim doing the same in the bath. But not only was I sitting in a hard, wooden chair, my feet were tied together with something that felt suspiciously like parcel tape and my hands were similarly bound behind my back. When I did finally open my eyes, it only got worse. Tim was next to me looking pale and confused ... by which I mean even more confused than usual. And Bastille and Lavache were sitting opposite us, both of them smoking.

The four of us were in a large, empty room that might once have been the dining-room of a grand château but was now empty and dilapidated. The floor was wooden and the walls white plaster, with no pictures or decorations. A broken chandelier hung from the ceiling. In fact quite a lot of the ceiling was hanging from the ceiling. Half of it seemed to be peeling off.

I had no idea how much time had passed since they'd knocked us out and bundled us into the back of a delivery van. An hour? A week? I couldn't see my watch – it was pinned somewhere behind me, along with the wrist it was on – so I twisted round and looked out of the window. The glass was so dust-covered that I could barely see outside, but from the light I would have said it was early evening. If so, we had been unconscious for about fifteen hours! I wondered where we were. Somewhere in the distance I thought I heard singing, the sound of a choir. But the music was foreign – and not French. It sounded vaguely religious, which made me think of churches. And that made me think of funerals. I just hoped they weren't singing for us.

"Good evening," Bastille muttered. He hadn't changed out of the dirty linen suit he had been wearing when we met him the day before. It was so crumpled now that I wondered if he had slept in it.

"What time is it?" Tim asked.

"It is time for you to talk!" Bastille blew a cloud of smoke into Tim's face.

Tim coughed. "You know those things can damage your health!" he remarked.

Not quickly enough, I thought. But I said nothing.

"It is *your* health that should concern you, my friend," Bastille replied.

"I'm perfectly well, thank you," Tim said.

"I mean – your health if you fail to tell us what we want to know!" Bastille's green eyes flared. He was even uglier when he was angry. "You have put us to a great deal of trouble," he went on. "We've searched you and this morning we searched your room. Are you going to tell us where it is?"

"It's on the top floor of the hotel!" Tim exclaimed.

"Not the room!" Bastille swore and choked on his cigarette. "I am talking about the packet that you were given by Marc Chabrol."

"The ex-steward," Lavache added. He giggled, and, looking at his ape-like hands, I suddenly knew how Chabrol had managed to "fall" under a train.

I'd said nothing throughout all this. I was just glad that I'd decided not to bring the packet with us. The two men must have searched Tim and me while we were unconscious. They had found nothing and it looked like they weren't going to go back and search the hotel room a second time.

"He gave us a cup of coffee," Tim was saying. "But we drank it. Unless you're talking about … wait a minute…"

"Who *are* you people?" I cut in. I didn't want him to say any more. So long as we had the sachet, they wouldn't kill us. They needed to know where it was. But the moment they heard it was hidden in the toilet, we were dead. That much was certain. I would just have to keep them talking and hope for the best. "Look…" I went on. "The steward didn't give us anything. We're just here on holiday."

"*Non, non, non!*" Bastille shook his head. "Do not try lying to me, *mon petit ami*. I know that your brother is a private detective. I also know that he was sent to Paris by Interpol. I know that he is working on a special assigment." His face turned ugly, which, with his face, wasn't difficult. "Now I want you to tell me how much you know and who gave you your information."

"But I don't know anything!" Tim wailed.

He'd never spoken a truer word in his life. Tim knew nothing about any special assignment. He'd have had trouble telling anyone his own shoe size. And he also hadn't realized that this was all his fault. If only he'd kept his mouth shut on the train! He'd told Jed Mathis and the old woman that he was working for Interpol. Could one of them have passed it on? Jed Mathis…?

Beware the mad American...

It was too late to worry about that. I realized that Tim was still talking. He had told them everything. The competition on the yoghurt pot. The free weekend. The truth.

"He's right," I admitted. "We're just tourists. We're not working for anyone."

"It was a strawberry yoghurt!" Tim burbled. "Bestlé yoghurts. They're only eighty calories each..."

"We don't know anything!" I said.

Bastille and Lavache moved closer to each other and began to mutter in low, dark voices. I couldn't understand a word they were saying, but somehow I didn't like the sound of it. I tried to break free from the chair but it was useless. Things weren't looking good. By now they must have realized that they were wrong about us, that we were exactly what we said. But they weren't just going to order us a taxi and pretend the whole thing had never happened. As they're always saying in the old movies ... we knew too much. I still had no idea who they were or what they were doing, but we knew their names and had seen their faces. That was enough.

The two men straightened up. "We have decided that we believe you," Bastille said.

"That's terrific!" Tim exclaimed.

"So now we are going to kill you."

"Oh!" His face fell.

Lavache walked to the far side of the room and I strained my neck to watch him. He reached out with both hands and suddenly a whole section of the wall slid to one side. I realized now that it wasn't a wall at all but a set of floor-to-ceiling doors. There was another room on the other side, filled with activity, and at that moment I realized what this was all about. Perhaps I should have guessed from the start.

Drugs.

The other room was a laboratory. I could see metal tables piled high with white powder. More white powder being weighed on complicated electronic scales. White powder being spooned into plastic bags. There were about half-a-dozen people working there, young men and women with dirty faces but pristine laboratory coats. They were handling the white powder in complete silence, as if they knew that it was death they were carrying in their hands and that if it heard them it would somehow find them out.

Lavache lumbered into the room, vanishing from sight. When he reappeared, he was holding something which he handed to Bastille. Right then I was more scared than I've ever been in my life, and you know me ... I don't scare easily. But suddenly I remembered that I was thirteen years old, that I hadn't started shaving yet and that my mother (who'd been shaving for years) was thousands of miles away. I was so scared I almost wanted to cry.

Bastille was holding a bottle of pills.

He approached Tim first. "These are super-strength," he said. "I think five of them will be enough."

"No, thank you," Tim said. "I haven't got a headache."

"They're not headache pills, Tim," I said.

Bastille grabbed hold of Tim and forced his mouth open. He had counted five pills into the palm of his hand and I watched, powerless, as he forced them down Tim's throat. Then he turned and began to walk towards me.

"They don't taste very nice!" I heard Tim say, but then I'd gone crazy, rocking back and forth, yelling, kicking with my feet, trying to tear apart the parcel tape around my wrists. It was useless. I felt Lavache grab hold of my shoulders while at the same time, Bastille took hold of my chin. I don't know what was worse. Feeling his bony fingers against my face or knowing there was nothing I could do as he forced my mouth open. His right hand came up and the next moment there were four or five pills on my tongue. They had an evil taste. I drew a breath, meaning to spit them out, but his hand was already over my mouth, almost suffocating me. I screamed silently and felt the pills trickle down the back of my throat. I almost felt them drop into the pit of my stomach. Then Bastille pulled his hand clear and my head sank forward. I said nothing. I thought I was dead. I thought he had killed me.

Things happened very quickly after that. It seemed to me that the lights in the room had brightened and that somebody had turned up the heating. My eyes were hurting. And then the walls began to revolve, slowly at first, like the start of a ride at a funfair. But there was nothing fun about this. Drugs are poison and I was sure I had just been given a lethal overdose. I was sweating. I tried to speak but my tongue refused to move; anyway, my mouth was too dry.

I heard the parcel tape being ripped off and felt my hands come free. Lavache was standing behind me. I tried to look at him, but my head lolled uselessly. He pulled me off the chair and carried me outside. Bastille followed with Tim.

There was a white van waiting for us in an enclosed courtyard – we could have been any-where. I looked back at the house we had just left. It was a grey building, three storeys high. Most of its paint had flaked off and there were scorch marks, as if it had been involved in a fire. About half the windows were shattered. Others had been bricked in. The place looked derelict. I guessed it was supposed to.

I was bundled into the van and the next moment the engine started up, roaring at me like a mechanical beast. I almost expected it to come bursting through the floor, to gobble me up. The noise hammered at my ears and I groaned. Tim was thrown in next to me. The doors slammed. My stomach heaved. We were off.

There was a small window set in the door and I managed to stagger over to it and pull myself onto my knees to look out. But it was hard to see anything. The world was spinning faster now, tilting from side to side. I just made out a series of letters in red neon, but it seemed to take me for ever to work out the three words they formed:

THE FRENCH CONFECTION

The van turned a corner and I lost my balance. Before I fell, I caught a glimpse of a blue star ... on a flag or perhaps on the side of a building. Then the sound of the van's engine rose up again and swallowed me. The floor hit me in the face. Or maybe it was me who had hit the floor. I no longer knew the difference.

The journey took an hour ... a month ... a year. I no longer had any idea. What was the stuff they had given me? Whatever it was, it was taking over, killing me. I could feel it happening, an inch at a time. The van stopped. Hands that no longer belonged to bodies pulled us out. Then the pavement slapped me in the face, there was another scream from the engine and suddenly I knew that we were alone.

"Tim…?" I gasped the word. But Tim was no longer there. He had turned into some horrible animal with sixteen eyes, tentacles and…

I forced myself to concentrate, knowing that it was the drug that was doing it to me. The image dissolved and there he was again. My brother.

"Nick…" He staggered to his feet. All three of them. Things weren't back to normal yet.

The sky changed from red to blue to yellow to green. I stood up as well.

"Must get help," I said.

Tim groaned.

We were back in the centre of Paris. It was late at night. And Paris had never looked like this before.

There was the Seine but the water had gone, replaced by red wine that glowed darkly in the moonlight. It was twisting its way underneath the bridges, but now that I looked more closely, I saw that they had changed too. They had become huge sticks of French bread. There was a sudden buzzing. A Bateau Mouche had suddenly sprouted huge blue wings and legs. It leapt out of the water and onto one of the bridges, tearing a great chunk out with a hideous, hairy mouth before spiralling away into the night.

The ground underneath my feet had gone soft

and I realized I was sinking into it. With a cry I lifted one foot and saw that the tar had melted and was dripping off my trainer. Except the tar was yellow, not black.

"It's cheese!" I shouted. And it was. The entire street had turned into cheese – soft, ripe, French cheese. I gasped for air, choking on the smell. At the same time, the cheese pulled me into it. Another few seconds and I would be sucked underneath the surface.

"Nick!" Tim called out.

And then the cheese was gone as he pointed with an arm that was now a mile long. There was a snail coming down the Boulevard. No … not one snail but a thousand of them, each one the size of a house, slithering along ahead of the traffic, leaving a grey, slimy trail behind them. At one corner, the traffic lights had gone red and all the snails were squeaking at each other, a fantastic traffic jam of snails. At the same time, I heard what sounded like a gigantic burp and a frog, the size of a bus, bounded across my vision, leaping over a building. But the frog was missing its legs. It was supporting itself on giant crutches.

The world twisted, heaved, broke up and then reformed with all the pieces in different positions: a jigsaw in the hands of a destructive child.

Suddenly we were surrounded by grinning stone figures, jabbering and staring at us with empty stone eyes. I recognized them: the gargoyles from Notre Dame. There must have been a hundred of them. One of them was sitting on Tim's shoulder like a grey chimpanzee. But Tim didn't seem to have noticed it.

Light. Car lights. Everywhere. A horn sounded. I had stepped into the road – but it didn't matter because the cars were the size of matchboxes. They were all Citroëns. Every one of them. And they were being followed by cyclists. The Tour de France had come early that year. All the cyclists were smoking cigarettes.

Tim was clutching a streetlamp. Now he was wearing a striped jersey and a beret and there was a string of onions hanging from his side. *"Je suis,"* he said. *"Tu es, il est…"*

I opened my mouth to reply.

Crash! Crash! Crash!

I saw it before he did. Perhaps he didn't see it at all. Even now, with the drug pumping through my body, I knew that it wasn't real, that I was hallucinating. But it made no difference. As far as I was concerned, everything I saw was real. And if it was real, it could kill me. It could step on me. It could crush me.

The Eiffel Tower! On our first day in Paris we had crossed the city to visit it. Now the Eiffel Tower was coming to visit us. There it was, walking across Paris, swinging one iron foot, then the next, moving like some sort of giant, four-legged crab. One of its feet came down in a pancake stall. Wood shattered. Pancakes flew in all directions. Somebody screamed.

The cheese was getting softer. I was sinking into a boulevard of Brie, a dual carriageway of Camembert. The squirming yellow slipped round my waist, rose over my shoulder and twisted round my neck. I didn't even try to fight. I'd had enough. I waited for it to pull me under.

I thought I was going to die and if I'd waited another minute I might well have. But just then I heard what I thought was an owl, hooting in my ear. At the same time, I found myself staring at a face I knew. A dark-haired man in a grey-coloured suit. I became aware of a blue flashing light which either belonged to a dragon or a police car. I looked up and saw something driving out of the moon, flying through the sky towards me. An ambulance.

"Don't go to sleep!" a voice commanded. "Don't go to sleep! Don't go to sleep!"

But it was too late. I went to sleep.

For ever.

THE MAD AMERICAN

"You're lucky to be alive," the man said.

It was two days later. I don't want to tell you about those two days. I'd spent both of them in hospital in Paris and all I can say is, if you've ever had your stomach pumped, you'll know there are plenty of things you can do that are more fun. I don't remember much about the first day. The next day, I felt like a spin-drier that's been left on too long. All I'd eaten in the entire time was a little bread and water. Fortunately, the water didn't have bubbles. I don't think I could have managed the bubbles.

And now, here I was in the headquarters of Sûreté, the French police force. It's funny how police stations are the same the whole world over. This may have been grander and smarter than New Scotland Yard. The curtains were velvet and the pictures on the wall showed some grey-haired Frenchman in a suit rather than our own grey-haired Queen in a crown. But it still smelled the same.

Tim was sitting next to me. He was the colour of the yoghurt that had brought us here in the first place, with eyes like crushed strawberries. His hair was dishevelled and he looked like he hadn't slept in a month. I was going to say something but decided against it. I probably looked just as bad.

We were in the office of the Chief of Police – a man called Christien Moire. I knew because I'd seen the name and title on the door. It was on his desk too. Maybe he was worried he was going to forget it. He was the man in the grey suit whom I'd seen standing outside Le Chat Gris, the man who had been talking to the receptionist and who had later taken our photograph. Things were beginning to add up even if I still had no idea of the sum total.

"Another one hour and it would have been too late," Moire went on. He spoke English as if he had no idea what he was saying, lingering on every word. He had the sort of accent you get in bad television plays: *Anuzzer wan our an' eet would 'ave bin too late*. I hope you get the idea. "You were very lucky," he added.

"Sure," I muttered. "And we'd have been even luckier if you'd arrived a couple of hours before."

Moire shrugged. "I'm sorry," he said. But his dark, empty eyes looked about as apologetic as

69

two lumps of ice. "We had no idea you had been taken," he went on.

"Who are you?" Tim demanded. "You call yourself the Sûreté. But what exactly are you sure about?"

"The Sûreté," Moire repeated, "is the French police force. I am the head of a special unit fighting the traffic in …"

"…drugs." I completed the sentence.

"*Exactement*. I have to say that you and your brother seem to have turned up in the wrong place at the wrong time. If I hadn't been watching you…"

"You were at the hotel," I said. "I saw you outside. You had a camera…"

"Is that your hobby?" Tim asked. "Photography?"

Christien Moire stared at Tim through narrow eyes. He obviously hadn't ever met anyone like him before. "Le Chat Gris has been under surveillance," he said. "Perhaps I should explain…"

"Perhaps you should," I said.

Moire lit a Gauloise. It's a funny thing about the French. Not only do they all smoke, but they smoke the most horrible cigarettes in the world. Forget about the health warning on the packet. The smoke from Moire's cigarette was so thick, you could have printed it on that.

"For some time now," he began, "we have been

aware of a drug-smuggling operation. Somebody has been moving drugs to London … using the trains under the channel. We still don't know how they're doing it. We have searched the trains from top to bottom but we have found nothing. Worse still, we do not know who they are."

"Is there anything you *do* know?" I asked.

Moire glanced at me with unfriendly eyes. "We know only the code-name of the man behind the operation," he replied.

"The Mad American," I said.

That surprised Moire, but he tried not to show it. "The drugs arrive from Marseilles," he went on. "They are weighed and packaged somewhere in Paris. Then the Mad American arranges for them to be sent to London. We've been working with the English police to try to stop them. So far we have had no success in London. But in Paris we had one lucky break."

"Le Chat Gris," I said.

"Yes, we learned that the hotel is sometimes used by the Mad American. When dealers arrive from London to buy his drugs, that is where they stay. He meets them there. They pay him the money and then his two associates – Jacques Bastille and Luc Lavache – arrange for the drugs to be sent on the train."

"So *that's* why you photographed us!" I said. "You thought we'd come to Paris to buy drugs!"

"I know it sounds unlikely," Moire said. "An

English kid and his idiotic brother –"

"Nick isn't idiotic!" Tim protested.

"We became interested in you the moment you reported that Bastille and Lavache had attempted to kill you," Moire went on. "I ordered the photograph to be taken so that we could check you against our criminal files."

"But if you thought we were criminals, why did you let us go in the first place?" I asked. It had puzzled me at the time, the policeman suddenly changing his mind and telling us we could leave.

"The answer to that is simple," Moire said. "We still had no idea what part you had to play in all this, but you had mentioned Le Chat Gris and that was enough. It was important that the Mad American should not be aware that the police were involved. I personally ordered your release, and at the same time I made sure that we kept you under – how do you say? – surveillance. This was very lucky for you, considering how things turned out."

"You were following us."

"Yes. I saw you go back to the hotel, and minutes later I saw the van with the two men who knocked you out and kidnapped you. We followed the van but unfortunately lost it in traffic…"

"…so you don't know where we were taken."

"No. But I knew that you were in danger and

I had every gendarme in Paris looking out for you. One of them saw you and radioed HQ. By that time they had pumped you with enough drugs to kill a horse."

"Why would they want to kill a horse?" Tim asked.

Moire ignored him. "We only got to you in the nick of time. Another ten minutes, and the two of you would now be in Père Lachaise."

"You mean, another hotel," Tim said.

"No. Père Lachaise is a cemetery."

"OK. You saved us, Monsieur Moire," I said. "But now, if you don't mind, I'm heading back to the hotel, packing and leaving for London."

"That's right, Monsieur Loire," Tim agreed. "We're out of here!"

"I'm afraid not." Moire hadn't raised his voice. If anything, he had done the exact opposite. But that's the thing about the French. When they're being really nasty, they don't shout. They whisper. "You realize that I could have you arrested?" he asked.

I almost laughed. "What for?" I demanded.

"You were found in the middle of Paris, full of drugs," the police chief explained. He sounded almost reasonable. "Two English tourists who decided to experiment with these forbidden substances..."

"That's a complete lie!" I exclaimed.

"Yes!" Tim agreed. "We're not tourists!"

"And then there is the matter of the Bateau Mouche…" Moire continued. "You jumped off a bridge, endangering the lives of the people on the boat. This could also prove to be drug-related."

"What do you want, Moire?" I demanded.

Moire leaned forward. His face could have been carved out of stone. Even the cigarette smoke seemed to have solidified. "There are two things we wish to find out," he said. "First, who is the Mad American?"

"Why don't you ask Bastille and Lavache?" I demanded.

"They wouldn't tell us anything. And if we did arrest them, it would only let their boss know that we were getting close … and that would ruin everything. The second thing we wish to know is, how are they smuggling the drugs across the Channel? As I have told you, we have searched the train many times … but with no success. These packets of white powder – they must be somewhere. But…" He smacked his forehead with the palm of his hand. "It is infuriating!"

"What do you want us to do?" I asked.

"I want you to go back to the hotel," Moire replied. "It will be as if nothing has happened."

"Why?"

"Because you can be useful to me … on the inside. My men will continue to watch you.

74

You'll be completely safe. But maybe you can find the answers to the questions. And if there is anything to report…"

"Forget it!" I snapped.

"Right!" Tim nodded. "Bestlé only paid for four days. We can't possibly afford it."

"Bestlé?" For the first time Moire looked puzzled. "Who is Bestlé?"

"It doesn't matter," I replied. "We're British citizens. You can't blackmail us!"

"You don't think so?" Moire almost smiled. "You are Europeans now, my friend. And if you don't do exactly as I tell you, let me assure you that you will be spending a great deal of time inside a European jail."

I wanted to argue, but I could see there was no point. The last person to argue with Christien Moire probably found himself with a one-way ticket to Devil's Island.

He knew he'd beaten me. "Go back to Le Chat Gris and wait for further instructions," he said. "Don't worry about the bill. I will see to it."

"And what if we get killed?" I asked.

"My department will pay for the funeral too."

I sank back in my chair. There was nothing I could say. Not in French. Not in English. It really wasn't fair.

* * *

And that was how we found ourselves, a few hours later, back in our room at Le Chat Gris. As I'd walked back into the hotel, I'd known how those French aristocrats must have felt as they took their last steps towards the guillotine. The receptionist had almost fallen off his chair when he saw us and he'd been on the telephone before we'd reached the lift. The Mad American would have presumed we were dead. Now he'd know he was wrong. How long would it take him to correct his mistake?

Tim sat down on the bed. He was actually looking quite cheerful, which made me feel even worse. "Maybe this isn't so bad, Nick," he said.

"Tim!" I cried. "How bad can it get?"

"We're working for the French police now," he said. "This could be good for business! *Tim Diamond Inc … London and Paris*. That'll look good on the door."

"It'll look even better on your gravestone," I said. "Don't you understand, Tim?" We're not working for anyone! Christien Moire was lying through his teeth!"

"You mean … he isn't a policeman?"

"Of course he's a policeman. But he doesn't want us to work for him. He's using us!" I'd taken a guidebook of Paris out of my case. Now I sat down next to Tim. "Moire wants to find out the identity of the Mad American," I explained. "What's the best way to do that?"

"Just ask for Tim Diamond…"

"Just *use* Tim Diamond. He's sent us back here because he knows that our turning up again will panic the Mad American. He's already tried to kill us twice. He's certain to try again – and this time Moire will be watching. He's using us as bait in a trap, Tim. The Mad American kills us. Moire gets the Mad American. It's as simple as that."

I opened the guidebook. "I'm not sitting here, waiting to be shot," I said.

"Where do you want to be shot?" Tim asked.

"I don't want to be shot anywhere! That's why I'm going to find the Mad American before he finds us." I started to thumb through the pages. I still didn't know what I was looking for, but I had a good idea. "After we were knocked out, we were taken to the Mad American's headquarters," I said.

"But we were knocked out!" Tim said. "We didn't see anything."

"We didn't see much," I agreed. "But there were some clues. A blue star. Some words in a shop window – THE FRENCH CONFECTION. And when we were tied up, I heard something. Music. Singing."

"Do you think that was the Mad American?"

"No, Tim. It was coming from a building nearby." I stopped, trying to remember what I had heard. "It wasn't French singing," I said. "It was different… It was foreign."

Sitting next to me on the bed, Tim was making a strange noise. I thought for a moment that he had stomach-ache. Then I realized he was trying to hum the tune.

"That's right, Tim," I said. "It was something like that. Only a bit more human."

Tim stopped. I tried to think. How had the singing gone? It had been sad and somehow dislocated. A choir and a single male voice. At times it had been more like wailing than singing. Remembering it now made me think of a church. Was that it? Had it been religious music? But if so, what religion?

I'm not sure what happened first. The thought seemed to come into my mind at exactly the same moment as I found myself looking at the words *The Jewish Quarter* in the guidebook in my hands.

"Jewish music!" I exclaimed.

"Jewish?"

"The music that we heard, Tim. It was coming from a synagogue!"

Tim's eyes lit up. "You think we were taken to Jerusalem?"

"No, Tim. We were in Paris. But there's an area of Paris that's full of synagogues." I waved the book at him. "Le Marais. That's what it's called. The Jewish sector of Paris…"

"But how big is it?" Tim asked.

I read the page in front of me:

Originally a swamp, the Marais has grown to become one of the most fashionable areas of Paris. Its narrow streets are filled with shops and boutiques including some of the city's most elegant cafés and cake shops. The Marais is home to the Jewish quarter with numerous synagogues and kosher restaurants based around the Rue des Rosiers.

There was a map showing the area. It only had a couple of dozen roads. "It doesn't look too big," I said. "And at least we know what we're looking for. The French Confection."

"But what *is* The French Confection, Nick?"

"I think it must be a shop. Maybe it sells cakes or sweets or something. But once we've found it, we'll know we're right next to the factory. Find the sign and we'll have found the Mad American."

"And then?"

"Then we call Moire."

We slipped out of Le Chat Gris down the fire escape, dodging past Moire's men who were waiting for us at the front of the hotel. Then we dived into the nearest Metro station and headed north.

It was a short walk from the station to the start of Le Marais – the Place Vendôme, one of those Paris squares where even the trees manage to look expensive. From there we headed down towards a big, elegant building that turned out to be the Picasso museum. I'd studied Picasso at school. He's the guy who painted women with eyes in the sides of their necks and tables with legs going the wrong way. It's called surrealism. Maybe I should have taken Tim in, as he's pretty surreal himself. But we didn't have time.

We backtracked and found ourselves in a series of long, narrow streets with buildings rising five storeys on both sides. But I knew we were on the right track. There was no singing, but here and there I saw blue stars – the same stars I had glimpsed as I was bundled into the van. I knew what it was now: the six-pointed Star of David. There was one in every kosher food store and restaurant in the area.

We'd been following the Rue des Rosiers – the one I'd read about in the guidebook – but with no sign of the building where we'd been held. So now we started snaking up and down, taking the first on the right and the next on the left and so on. It was a pretty enough part of Paris, I'll say that for it. Tim had even forgotten our mission and stopped once or twice to take photographs. We'd been chased and threatened at knife-point. We'd been kidnapped, drugged and threatened again – this time by the French police. And he *still* thought we were on holiday!

And then, suddenly, we were there.

It was on one of the main streets of the area – the Rue de Sevigny. I recognized it at once: the burnt face of the building, the broken windows, the ugly chimney stacks... And there was the archway that we had driven through. There was a courtyard on the other side which was where the white van had been parked. I stood there in the sunlight, with people strolling past on the pavements, some carrying shopping bags, others pushing prams. And none of them knew. The biggest drug factory in Paris was right in front of them, just sitting there between a café and a cake shop, right in the middle of the Marais. I couldn't believe I had found it so easily. It was hard to believe it was there at all.

"Nick...!" Tim whispered.

I grabbed hold of him and pulled him down behind a parked car as Bastille and Lavache appeared, coming out of the front door and walking across the courtyard. Each of them had a heavy box in their hands. Another shipment on its way out! It made me angry that anyone should be dumb enough to want to buy drugs and angrier still that these two grim reapers would be getting richer by selling them.

"What do we do now?" Tim whispered.

"Now we call Moire," I said.

"Right!" Tim straightened up. "Let's ask in there!"

Before I could stop him he had walked across the pavement and into the cake shop. There was the sign in the window that I had seen from the van. THE FRENCH CONFECTION. Why did the name bother me? Why did I feel it was connected with something or someone I had seen? It was too late to worry about it now. Tim was already inside. I followed him in.

I found myself in a long, narrow shop with a counter running down one wall. Everywhere I looked there were cakes and croissants, bowls of coloured almonds and tiny pots of jam. The very air smelt of sugar and flour. On the counter stood one of the tallest wedding cakes I had ever seen: six platforms of swirly white icing with a marzipan bride and groom looking air-sick up on the top. There was a bead curtain at the back and now it rattled as the owner of the shop passed through, coming out to serve us. And of course I knew her. I'd met her on the train.

Erica Nice.

She stopped behind the counter, obviously as surprised to see us as we were to see her.

"You…!" she began.

"Mrs Nice!" Tim gurgled. I wondered how he had managed to remember her name. "We need to use your telephone. To call the police."

"I don't think so, Tim," I said.

Even as I spoke I was heading back towards the door. But I was already too late. Erica's hand came up and this time it wasn't holding an almond slice. It was the biggest gun I'd ever seen. Bigger than the wrinkled hand that held it. Its muzzle was as ugly as the smile on the old woman's face.

"But ... but ... but..." Tim stared.

"Erica Nice," I said. "I suppose I should have guessed. Madame Erica Nice. Say it fast and what do you get?"

"Madamericanice?" Tim suggested.

"Mad American," I said. "She's the one behind the drug racket, Tim. When we met her, she must have been checking the route. That's why she was on the train. And that's how Bastille and Lavache knew we were in Paris."

Erica Nice snarled at us. "Yes," she said. "I have to travel on the train now and then to keep an eye on things. Like that idiot steward – Marc Chabrol. He was scared. And scared people are no use to me."

"So you pushed him under a train," I said.

She shrugged. "I would have preferred to stab him. I did have my knitting needles, but unfortunately I was halfway through a woollen jumper. Pushing was easier."

"And what now?" I asked. I wondered if she was going to shoot us herself or call her two thugs to finish the job for her. At the same time, I took a step forward, edging my way towards the counter and the giant wedding cake.

"Those idiots – Jacques and Luc – should have got rid of you when they had the chance," Erica hissed. "This time they will make no mistakes."

She turned to press a switch set in the wall. Presumably it connected the shop with the factory next door.

I leapt forward and threw my entire weight against the cake.

Erica half turned. The gun came up.

The door of the shop burst open, the glass smashing.

And as Erica Nice gave a single shrill scream and disappeared beneath about ten kilograms of wedding cake, Christien Moire and a dozen gendarmes hurled themselves into the shop. At the same time, I heard the blare of sirens as police cars swerved into the road from all directions.

I turned to Moire. "You followed us here?"

Moire nodded. "Of course. I had men on all sides of the hotel."

Erica Nice groaned and tried to fight her way out of several layers of sponge, jam and butter cream. Tim leaned forward and scooped up a fragment of white icing. He popped it into his mouth.

"Nice cake," he said.

THE WHITE CLIFFS

The next day, Christien Moire drove us up to Calais and personally escorted us onto the ferry. It would have been easier to have taken the train, of course. But somehow Tim and I had had enough of trains.

It had been a good week for Moire. Jacques Bastille and Luc Lavache had both been arrested. So had Erica Nice. The drug factory had been closed down and more arrests were expected. No wonder Moire wanted us out of the way. He was looking forward to promotion and maybe the Croix de Guerre or whatever medal French heroes get pinned to their right nipple. The last thing Moire needed was Tim and me hanging around to tell people the part we had played.

Moire stopped at the quay and handed us our tickets as well as a packed lunch for the crossing. "France is in your debt," he said, solemnly, and before either of us could stop him he had grabbed hold of Tim and planted a kiss on both cheeks.

Tim went bright red. "I know I cracked the case," he muttered. "But let's not get too friendly..."

"It's just the French way," I said. Even so, I made sure I shook hands with Moire. I didn't want him getting too close.

"I wish you a good journey, my friends," Moire said. "And this time, perhaps you will be careful what you say while you are on the ship!"

"We won't be saying anything," I promised. I'd bought Tim a Tintin book at the harbour bookstall. He could read that on the way home.

Moire smiled. *"Au revoir,"* he said.

"Where?" Tim asked. I'd have to translate it for him later.

We were about halfway home, this time chopping up and down on the Channel, when Tim suddenly looked up from the Tintin book. "You know," he said. "We never did find out how Erica Nice was smuggling the drugs on the train."

"Haven't you guessed?" I sighed and pulled out the blue sugar sachet that had started the whole thing. It was the sachet Tim had been given at the Gare du Nord. Somehow I'd never quite got round to opening it. I did so now.

There was a spoonful of white powder inside.

"Sugar?" Tim muttered.

"I don't think so, Tim," I replied. "This is just one sachet. But Erica Nice was transporting thousands of them every day on the train. A little parcel of drugs. One dose, already weighed and perfectly concealed." I tore open the packet and held it up. The powder was caught in the wind and snatched away. I watched it go, a brief flurry of white as it skimmed over the handrail and disappeared into the grey water of the English Channel.

"Do you think we ought to tell Moire?" Tim asked.

"I expect he's worked it out for himself," I said.

In the distance I could see the white cliffs of Dover looming up. We had only been away for a week but somehow it seemed a lot longer. I was glad to be home.

Tim was still holding the packed lunch that Moire had given us. Now he opened it. The first thing he took out was a strawberry yoghurt.

"Very funny," I said.

The yoghurt followed the drugs into the channel. Then we went downstairs to order fish and chips.

I KNOW WHAT YOU DID LAST WEDNESDAY

AN INVITATION

I like horror stories – but not when they happen to me. If you've read my other adventures, you'll know that I've been smothered in concrete, thrown in jail with a dangerous lunatic, tied to a railway line, almost blown up, chased through a cornfield dodging machine-gun bullets, poisoned in Paris ... and all this before my fourteenth birthday. It's not fair. I do my homework. I clean my teeth twice a day. Why does everyone want to kill me?

But the worst thing that ever happened to me began on a hot morning in July. It was the first week of the summer holidays and there I was, as usual, stuck with my big brother Tim, the world's most unsuccessful private detective. Tim had just spent a month helping with security at the American Embassy in Grosvenor Square and even now I'm not sure how he'd decided that there was a bomb in the ambassador's car. Anyway, just as the ambassador was about to get in, Tim had grabbed hold of him and hurled him out of the way – which would have been heroic if there had been a bomb (there wasn't) and if Tim hadn't managed to throw the unfortunate man in front of a passing bus. The ambassador was now in hospital. And Tim was out of work.

So there we were at the breakfast table with Tim reading the morning post while I counted out the cornflakes. We were down to our last packet and it had to last us another week. That allowed us seventeen flakes each but as a treat I'd allowed Tim to keep the free toy. There was a handful of letters that morning and so far they'd all been bills.

"There's a letter from Mum," Tim said.

"Any money?"

"No…"

He quickly read the letter. It was strange to think that my mum and dad were still in Australia and that I would have been with them if I hadn't slipped off the plane and gone to stay with Tim. My dad was a door-to-door salesman, selling doors. He had a house in Sydney with three bedrooms and forty-seven doors. It had been two years now since I had seen him.

"Mum says you're welcome to visit," Tim said. "She says the door is always open."

"Which one?" I asked.

He picked up the last letter. I could see at once that this wasn't a bill. It came in a square, white envelope made out of the sort of paper that only comes from the most expensive trees. The address was handwritten: a fountain-pen, not a biro. Tim weighed it in his hand. "I wonder what this is," he said.

"It's an envelope, Tim," I replied. "It's what letters come in."

"I mean … I wonder who it's from!" He smiled. "Maybe it's a thank-you letter from the American ambassador."

"Why should he thank you? You threw him under a bus!"

"Yes, but I sent him a bunch of grapes in hospital."

"Just open it, Tim," I said.

Tim grabbed hold of a knife, and – with a dramatic gesture – sliced open the mysterious envelope.

After we'd finished bandaging his left leg, we examined the contents. First, there was an invitation, printed in red ink on thick white card.

Dear Herbert, it began. Tim Diamond was, of course, only the name he called himself. His real name was Herbert Simple.

It has been many years since we met, but I would like to invite you to a reunion of old boys and girls from St Egbert's Comprehensive, which will take place from Wednesday 9th to Friday 11th July. I am sure you are busy but I am so keen to see you again that I will pay you £1,000 to make the journey to Scotland. I also enclose a ticket for the train.

Your old friend,
Rory McDougal

Crocodile Island, Scotland

Tim tilted the envelope. Sure enough, a first-class train ticket slid out onto the table.

"That's fantastic!" Tim exclaimed. "A first-class ticket to Scotland." He examined the ticket. "And back again! That's even better!"

"Wait a minute," I said. "Who is Rory McDougal?" But even as I spoke, I thought the name was familiar.

"We were at school together, in the same class. Rory was brilliant. He came first in maths. He was so clever, he passed all his exams without even reading the questions. After he left school, he invented the pocket calculator – which was just as well, because he made so much money he needed a pocket calculator to count it."

"McDougal Industries." Now I knew where I'd heard the name. McDougal had been in the newspapers. The man was a multi-Mcmillionaire.

"When did you last see him?" I asked.

"It must have been on prize-giving day, about

ten years ago," Tim said. "He went to university, I joined the police."

Tim had only spent a year with the police but in that time the crime rate had doubled. He didn't often talk about it but I knew that he had once put together an identikit picture that had led to the arrest of the Archbishop of Canterbury. He'd been transferred to the mounted police but that had only lasted a few weeks before his horse resigned. Then he'd become a private detective – and of course, *he* had hardly made millions. If you added up all the money Tim had ever made and put it in a bank, the bank wouldn't even notice.

"Are you going?" I asked.

Tim flicked a cornflake towards his mouth. It disappeared over his shoulder. "Of course I'm going," he said. "Maybe McNoodle will offer me a job. Head of Security on Alligator Island."

"Crocodile Island, Tim." I picked up the invitation. "What about me?"

"Sorry, kid. I didn't see your name on the envelope."

"Maybe it's under the stamp." Tim said nothing, so I went on, "You can't leave me here."

"Why not?"

"I'm only fourteen. It's against the law."

Tim frowned. "I won't tell if you won't tell."

"I will tell."

"Forget it, Nick. McStrudel is my old

schoolfriend. He went to my old school. It's my name on the envelope and you can argue all you like. But this time, I'm going alone."

We left King's Cross station on the morning of the 9th.

Tim sat next to the window, looking sulky. I was sitting opposite him. I had finally persuaded him to swap the first-class ticket for two second-class ones, which at least allowed me to travel free. You may think it strange that I should have wanted to join Tim on a journey heading several hundred miles north. But there was something about the invitation that bothered me. Maybe it was the letter, written in ink the colour of blood. Maybe it was the name – Crocodile Island. And then there was the money. The invitation might have sounded innocent enough, but why was McDougal paying Tim £1,000 to get on the train? I had a feeling that there might be more to this than a school reunion. And for that matter, why would anyone in their right mind want to be reunited with Tim?

I was also curious. It's not every day that you get to meet a man like Rory McDougal. Computers, camcorders, mobile phones and DVD players ... they all came stamped with the initials RM. And every machine that sold made McDougal a little richer.

Apparently the man was something of a

recluse. A few years back he'd bought himself an island off the Scottish coast, somewhere to be alone. There had been pictures of it in all the newspapers. The island was long and narrow with two arms jutting out and a twisting tail. Apparently, that was how it had got its name.

Tim didn't say much on the journey. To cheer him up, I'd bought him a *Beano* comic and perhaps he was having trouble with the long words. It took us about four hours to get to Scotland and it took another hour before I noticed. There were no signs, no frontier post, no man in a kilt playing the bagpipes and munching haggis as the train went past. It was only when the ticket collector asked us for our tickets and Tim couldn't understand a word he was saying that I knew we must be close. Sure enough, a few minutes later the train slowed down and Tim got out. Personally, I would have waited until the train had actually stopped, but I suppose he was over-excited.

Fortunately he was only bruised and we managed the short walk down to the harbour where an old fishing boat was waiting for us. The boat was called the *Silver Medal* and a small crowd of people were waiting to go on board.

"My God!" one of them exclaimed. "It's Herbert Simple! I never thought I'd see *him* again!"

The man who had spoken was fat and bald, dressed in a three-piece suit. If he ate much more, it would soon be a four-piece suit. His trousers were already showing the strain. His name, it turned out, was Eric Draper. He was a lawyer.

Tim smiled. "I changed my name," he announced. "It's Tim Diamond now."

They all had a good laugh at that.

"And who is he?" Eric asked. I suddenly realized he was looking at me.

"That's my kid brother, Nick."

"So what are you doing now ... Tim?" one of the women asked in a high-pitched voice. She had glasses and long, curly hair and such large teeth that she seemed to have trouble closing her mouth. Her name was Janet Rhodes.

Tim put on his "don't mess with me" face. Unfortunately, it just made him look seasick. "Actually," he drawled, "I'm a private detective."

"Really?" Eric roared with laughter. His suit shuddered and one of the buttons flew off. "I can't believe Rory invited you here too. As I recall, you were the stupidest boy at St Egbert's. I still remember your performance as Hamlet in the school play."

"What was so stupid about that?" I asked.

"Nothing. Except everyone else was doing Macbeth."

One of the other women stepped forward. She was small and drab-looking, dressed in a mousy coat that had seen better days. She was eating a chocolate flake. "Hello ... Tim!" she said shyly. "I bet you don't remember me!"

"Of course I remember you!" Tim exclaimed. "You're Lisa Beach!"

"No I'm not! I'm Sylvie Binns." She looked disappointed. "You gave me my first kiss behind the bike shed. Don't you remember?"

Tim frowned. "I remember the bike shed..." he said.

There was a loud blast from the boat and the captain appeared, looking over the side. He had one leg, one eye and a huge beard. All that was missing was the parrot and he could have got a job in any pantomime in town. "All aboard!" he shouted. "Departing for Crocodile Island!"

We made our way up the gangplank. The boat was old and smelly. So was the captain. The eight of us stood on the deck while he pulled up the anchor, and a few minutes later we were off, the engine rattling as if it was about to fall out of the boat. It occurred to me that the Silver Medal was a strange choice of boat for a multi-millionaire. What had happened to the deluxe yacht? But nobody else had noticed, so I said nothing.

Apart from Eric, Janet and Sylvie, there were three other people on board: two more women and another man, a fit-looking black guy dressed in jeans and a sweatshirt.

"That's Mark Tyler," Tim told me as we cut through the waves, leaving the mainland behind us. "He came first at sport at St Egbert's…"

I knew the name. Tyler had been in the British Olympic athletics team at Atlanta.

"He used to run to school and run home again," Tim went on. "He was so fast, he used to overtake the school bus. When he went cross-country running, he actually left the country, which certainly made the headmaster very cross. He's a brilliant sportsman!"

That just left the two other women.

Brenda Blake was an opera singer and looked it. Big and muscular, she had the sort of arms you'd expect to find on a Japanese wrestler – or perhaps around his belly.

Libby Goldman was big and blonde and worked in children's TV, presenting a television programme called *Libby's Lounge*. She sang, danced, juggled and did magic tricks … and all this before we'd even left the quay. It was a shame that in real life we couldn't turn her off.

The journey took about an hour, by which time the coast of Scotland had become just a grey smudge behind us. Slowly Crocodile Island sneaked up on us. It was about half a mile long, rising to a point at what must have been its "tail", with sheer cliffs sweeping down into the sea. There were six jagged pillars of rock at this end, making a landing impossible. But at the other end, in the shelter of the crocodile's arm, someone had built a jetty. As the boat drew in, I noticed a security camera watching us from above.

"Here we are, ladies and gentlemen," the captain announced from somewhere behind his beard. "I wish you all a very pleasant stay on Crocodile Island. I do indeed! I'll be coming back for you in a couple of days. My name is Captain Randle, by the way. Horatio Randle. It's been a pleasure having you lovely people on my boat. You remember me, now!"

"Aren't you coming with us?" Eric demanded.

"No, sir. I'm not invited," Captain Randle replied. "I live on the mainland. But I'll be back to collect you in a couple of days. I'll see you then!"

We disembarked. The boat pulled out and headed back the way it had come. The eight of us were left on the island, wondering what was going to happen next.

"So where's old Rory?" Brenda asked.

"Maybe we should walk up to the house," Sylvie suggested. She was the only one of them who didn't have a full-time job. She had told Tim that she was a housewife, and was carrying three photographs of her husband and three more of her house.

"Bit of a cheek," Eric muttered. From the look of him, walking wasn't something he did often.

"Best foot forward!" Janet said cheerily. Apparently she worked as a hairdresser, and her own hair was dancing in the wind. As indeed was Libby.

We walked. Sylvie might have called it a house but I would have said it was a castle that Rory had bought for himself on his island retreat. It was built out of grey brick: a grand, sprawling building with towers and battlements and even gargoyles gazing wickedly out of the corners. We reached the front door. It was solid oak, as thick as a tree and half as welcoming.

"I wonder if we should knock?" Tim asked.

"To hell with that!" Eric pushed and the door swung open.

We found ourselves in a great hall with a black and white floor, animal heads on the walls and a roaring fire in the hearth. A grandfather clock chimed four times. I looked at my watch – it was actually ten past three. I was already beginning to feel uneasy. Apart from the crackle of the logs and the ticking of the clock, the house was silent. It felt empty. No Rory, no Mrs Rory, no butler, no cook. Just us.

"Hello?" Libby called out. "Is there anyone at home?"

"It-doesn't-look-as-if-there's-anyone-here," Mark said. At least, I think that's what he said. Speaking was something else that he did very fast. Whole sentences came out of his mouth as a single word.

"This is ridiculous," Eric snapped. "I suggest we split up and try and find Rory. Maybe he's asleep upstairs."

So we all went our separate ways. Mark and Eric headed off through different doors. Libby Goldman went into the kitchen. Tim and I went upstairs. It was only now that we were inside it that I realized just how big this house was. It had five staircases, doors everywhere and so many corridors that we could have been walking through a maze. And if it looked like a castle from the outside, inside it was like a museum. There was more furniture than you'd find in a department store. Antique chairs and sofas stood next to cupboards and sideboards and tables of every shape and size. There were so many oil paintings that you could hardly see the walls. Rory also seemed to have a fondness for ancient weapons – I had only been in the place a few minutes but already I had seen crossbows and muskets and flintlock pistols mounted on wooden plaques. On the first floor there was a stuffed bear holding an Elizabethan gun ... a blunderbuss. The stairs and upper landing were covered in thick, red carpet which muffled every sound. In the distance I could hear Janet calling out Rory's name but it was difficult to say if she was near or far away. Suddenly we were lost and very much on our own.

We reached a corner where there was a suit of dull silver armour standing guard; a knight with a shield but no sword.

"I don't like it," I said.

"I think it's a very nice suit of armour," Tim replied.

"I'm not talking about the armour, Tim," I said. "I'm talking about the whole island. Why isn't there anyone here to meet us? And why did your friend send that old fishing boat to pick us up?"

Tim smiled. "Relax, kid," he said. "The house is a bit quiet, that's all. But my sixth sense would tell me if there was something wrong, and right now I'm feeling fine..."

Just then there was a high-pitched scream from another part of the second floor. It was Brenda. She screamed and screamed again.

"How lovely!" Tim exclaimed. "Brenda's singing for us! I think that's Mozart, isn't it?"

"It's not Mozart, Tim," I shouted, beginning to run towards the sound. "She's screaming for help! Come on!"

We ran down the corridor and round the corner. That was when we saw Brenda, standing in front of an open bedroom door. She had stopped screaming now but her face was white and her hands were tearing at her hair. At the same time, Libby and Sylvie appeared, coming up the stairs. And Eric was also there, pushing his way forward to see what the fuss was about.

Tim and I reached the doorway. I looked inside.

The room had a red carpet. It took me a couple of seconds to realize that the room had once had a yellow carpet. It was covered in blood. There was more blood on the walls and on the bed. There was even blood on the blood.

And there was McDougal. I'm afraid it was the end of the story for Rory. The sword that had killed him was lying next to him and I guess it must have been taken from the suit of armour.

Brenda screamed again and pulled out a handful of her own hair.

Eric stood back, gasping.

Libby burst into tears.

And Tim, of course, fainted.

There were just the eight of us, trapped on Crocodile Island. And I had to admit, our reunion hadn't got off to a very good start.

AFTER DARK

"It was horrible," Tim groaned. "It was horrible. Rory McPoodle ... he was in pieces!"

"I don't want to hear about it, Tim," I said. Actually, it was too late. He'd already told me twenty times.

"Why would anyone *do* that?" he demanded. "What sort of person would do that?"

"I'm not sure," I muttered. "How about a dangerous lunatic?"

Tim nodded. "You could be right," he said.

We were sitting in our bedroom. We knew it was the bedroom that McDougal had prepared for us because it had Tim's name on the door. There were seven bedrooms on the same floor, each one of them labelled for the arriving guests. This room was square, with a high ceiling and a window with a low balcony looking out over a sea that was already grey and choppy as the sun set and the evening drew in. There was a four-poster bed, a heavy tapestry and the sort of wallpaper that could give you bad dreams. There was also something else I'd noticed and it worried me.

"Look at this, Tim," I said. I pointed at the bedside table. "There's a telephone socket here – but no telephone. What does that tell you?"

"The last person who slept in this room stole the telephone?"

"Not exactly. I think the telephone has been taken to stop us making any calls."

"Why would anyone do that?"

"To stop us reporting the death of Rory McDougal to the police."

Tim considered. "You mean … someone knew we were coming…" he began.

"Exactly. And they also knew we'd be stuck here. At least until the boat came back."

It was a nasty thought. I was beginning to have lots of nasty thoughts, and the worst one was this: someone had killed Rory McDougal, but had it happened before we arrived on the island? Or had he been killed by one of the people from the boat? As soon as we had arrived at the house, we had all split up. For at least ten minutes nobody had known where anybody else was, which meant that any one of us could have found Rory and killed him before the others arrived.

Along with Tim and myself, there were

now six people on the island ... six and several halves if you counted Rory. Eric Draper, Janet Rhodes, Sylvie Binns, Mark Tyler, Brenda Blake and Libby Goldman. Tim hadn't seen any of them in ten years and knew hardly anything about them. Could one of them be a crazed killer? Could one of them have planned this whole thing?

I looked at my watch. It was ten to seven. We left the room and went back downstairs.

Eric Draper had called a meeting in the dining-room at seven o'clock. I don't know who had put him in charge but I guessed he had decided himself.

"He was head boy at school," Tim told me. "He was always telling everyone what to do. Even the teachers used to do what he said."

"What was Rory McDougal like as a boy?"

"Well ... he was young."

"That's very helpful, Tim. I mean ... was he popular?"

"Yes. Except he once had a big row with Libby Goldman. He tried to kiss her in biology class and she attacked him with a bicycle pump."

"But she wouldn't kill him just because of that, would she?"

"You should have seen where she put the bicycle pump!"

In fact Libby was alone in the dining-room when we arrived for the meeting. She was sitting in a chair at the end of a black, polished table that ran almost the full length of the room. Portraits of bearded men in different shades of tartan looked down from the walls. A chandelier hung from the ceiling.

She looked up as we came in. Her eyes were red. Either she had been crying or she had bad hay fever – and I hadn't noticed any hay on Crocodile Island. She was smoking a cigarette – or trying to. Her hands were shaking so much she had trouble getting it into her mouth.

"What are we going to do?" she wailed. "It's so horrible! I knew I shouldn't have accepted Rory's invitation!"

"Why did you?" I asked. "If you didn't like him…"

"Well … he's interesting. He's rich. I thought he might appear on my television programme – Libby's Lounge."

"I watch that!" Tim exclaimed.

"But it's a children's programme," Libby said.

Tim blushed. "Well … I mean … I've seen it. A bit of it."

"I've never heard of it," I muttered.

Libby's eyes went redder.

Then three of the others came in: Janet Rhodes, Mark Tyler and Brenda Blake.

"I've been trying to call the mainland on my mobile phone," Janet announced. "But I can't get a signal."

"I can't get a signal either," agreed Mark, speaking as quickly as ever. He sort of shimmered in front of me and suddenly he was sitting down.

"There is no signal on this island."

"And no phone in my room," Janet said.

"No phone in any room!" The singer was looking pale and scared. Of course, she was the one who had found the body. Looking at her, I saw that it would be a few months before she sang in a concert hall. She probably wouldn't have the strength to sing in the bath.

Somewhere a clock struck seven and Eric Draper waddled into the room. "Are we all here?" he asked.

"I'm here!" Tim called out, as helpful as ever.

"I think there's one missing," I said.

Eric Draper did a quick head count. At least everyone in the room still had their heads. "Sylvie isn't here yet," he said. He scowled. You could tell he was the sort of man who expected everyone to do exactly what he said. "We'll have to wait for her."

"She was always late for everything," Janet muttered. She had slumped into a chair next to Libby. "I don't know how she managed to come first in chemistry. She was always late for class."

"I saw her in her room a few moments ago," Mark said. "She was sitting on the bed. She looked upset."

"I'm upset!" Eric said. "We're all upset!

Well, let's begin without her." He cleared his throat as if we were the jury and he was about to begin his summing up. "We are clearly in a very awkward situation here. We've been invited to this island, only to discover that our host, Rory McDougal, has been murdered. We can't call the police because it would seem that there are no telephones and none of our mobiles can get a signal. Unless we can find a boat to get back to the mainland, we're stuck here until Captain Randle – or whatever his name was – arrives to pick us up. The only good news is that there's plenty of food in the house. I've looked in the kitchen. This is a comfortable house. We should be fine here."

"Unless the killer strikes again," I said.

Everyone looked at me. "What makes you think he'll do that?" Eric demanded.

"It's a possibility," I said. "And anyway, 'he' could be a 'she'."

I noticed Libby shivered when I said that – but to be frank she'd been shivering a lot recently.

"Did Rory invite you here too?" Mark asked.

"Not exactly. He invited Tim, and Tim couldn't leave me on my own at home. So I came along for the ride."

Eric scowled for a second time. Scowling suited him. "I wouldn't have said this place was suitable for children," he said.

"Murder isn't suitable for children," I agreed.

"But I'm stuck here with you and it seems to me that we've all been set up. No phones! That has to be on purpose. All the rooms were prepared for us, with our names on the doors. And now, like you say, we're stuck here. Suppose the killer is here too?"

"That's not possible," Brenda whispered. But she didn't sound like she believed herself.

"Maybe Rory wasn't murdered," Tim suggested. "Maybe it was an accident."

"You mean someone accidentally chopped him to pieces?" I asked.

Janet glanced at the door. She was looking nervous. A hairdresser having a bad hair day. "Perhaps we should go and find Sylvie," she suggested.

Nobody said anything. Then, as one, we hurried out of the room.

We went back upstairs. Sylvie's room was halfway down the corridor, two doors away from our own. It was closed. Tim knocked. There was no reply. "She could have fallen asleep," he said.

"Just open the door, Tim," I suggested.

He opened it. Sylvie's room was a similar size to ours but with more modern furniture, an abstract painting on the wall and two single beds. Her case was standing beside the wall, unopened. As my eyes travelled towards her, I noticed a twist of something silver lying in the middle of the yellow carpet. But I didn't have time to mention it.

Sylvie was lying on her back, one hand flung out. When I had first seen her I had thought her small and silent. Now she was smaller and dreadfully still. I felt Mark push past me, entering the room.

"Is she...?" he began.

"Yes," Tim said. "She's asleep."

"I don't think so, Tim," I said.

Eric went over to her and took her wrist between a podgy finger and thumb. "She has no pulse," he said. He leant over her. "She's not breathing."

Tim's mouth fell open. "Do you think she's ill?" he asked.

"She's dead, Tim," I said. Two murders in one day. And it wasn't even Tim's bedtime.

Libby burst into tears. It was getting to be a habit with her. At least Brenda didn't scream again. At this close range, I'm not sure my eardrums could have taken it.

"What are we going to do?" someone asked. I wasn't sure who it was and it didn't matter anyway. Because right then I didn't have any idea.

"It might have been a heart attack," Tim said. "Maybe the shock of what happened to Rory..."

Darkness had fallen on Crocodile Island. It had slithered across the surface of the sea and thrown itself over the house. Now and then a full moon came out from behind the clouds and for a moment the waves would ripple silver before disappearing into inky blackness. Tim and I were sitting on our four-poster bed. It looked like we were going to have to share it. Two posters each.

Maybe it had been a heart attack. Maybe she had died of fright. Maybe she'd caught a very bad case of flu. Everyone had their own ideas … but I knew better. I remembered the twist of silver I had seen on the carpet.

"Tim, what can you tell me about Sylvie Binns?" I asked.

"Not a lot." Tim fell silent. "She was good at chemistry."

"I know that."

"She used to go out with Mark. We always thought the two of them would get married, but in the end she met someone else. Mark ran all the way round England. That was his way of forgetting her."

Mark Tyler had been the last person to see Sylvie alive. I wondered if he really had forgotten her. Or forgiven her.

"Maybe she was ill before she came to the island," Tim muttered.

"Tim, I think she was poisoned," I said.

"Poisoned?"

I remembered my first sight of Sylvie, on the

quay. She had been eating a chocolate flake. "Sylvie liked sweets and chocolate," I said.

"You're right, Nick! Yes. She loved chocolate. She could never resist it. When Mark was going out with her, he took her on a tour of a chocolate factory. She even ate the tickets." Tim frowned. "But what's that got to do with anything?"

"There was a piece of silver paper on the floor in her room. I think it was the wrapper off a sweet or a chocolate. Don't you see? Someone knew she couldn't resist chocolate – so they left one in her room. Maybe on her pillow."

"And it wasn't almond crunch," Tim muttered darkly.

"More likely cyanide surprise," I said.

We got into bed. Tim didn't want to turn off the lights, but a few minutes later, after he had dozed off, I reached for the switch and lay back in the darkness. I needed to think. Sylvie had eaten a poisoned chocolate. I was sure of it. But had she been given it or had she found it in her room? If it was already in the room, it could have been left there before we arrived. But if she had been given it, then the killer must still be on the island. He or she might even be in the house.

There was a movement at the window.

At first I thought I'd imagined it, but propping myself up in the bed, I saw it again. There was somebody there! No – that was impossible.

We were on the first floor. Then I remembered. There was a terrace running round the outside of the house, connecting all the bedrooms.

There it was again. I stared in horror. There was a face staring at me from the other side of the glass, a hideous skull with hollow eyes and grinning, tombstone teeth. The bones glowed in the moonlight. Now I'll be honest with you. I don't scare easily. But right then I was frozen. I couldn't move. I couldn't cry out. I'm almost surprised I didn't wet the bed.

The skull hovered in front of me. I couldn't see a body. It had to be draped in black. It's a mask, I told myself. Someone is trying to frighten you with a joke-shop mask. Somehow, I managed to force back the fear. I jerked up in bed and threw back the covers. Next to me, Tim woke up.

"Is it breakfast already?" he asked.

I ignored him. I was already darting towards the window. But at that moment, the moon vanished behind another cloud and the darkness fell. By the time I had found the lock and opened the window, the man – or woman, whoever it was – had gone.

"What is it, Nick?" Tim demanded.

I didn't answer. But it seemed that whoever had killed Rory McDougal and Sylvie Binns was still on the island.

Which left me wondering – who was going to be next?

SEARCH PARTY

Janet Rhodes didn't make it to breakfast.

There were just the five of us, sitting in the kitchen with five bowls of Frosties and a steaming plate of scrambled eggs that Brenda had insisted on cooking but which nobody felt like eating. Libby had another cigarette in her mouth but everyone had complained so much that she wasn't smoking it. She was sucking it. Eric was still in his dressing-gown, a thick red thing with his initials – ED – embroidered on the pocket. Mark was wearing a track suit. A security camera winked at us from one corner of the room. There were a lot of security cameras on the island. But none of us felt even slightly secure.

"What are we going to do?" Brenda asked. I got the feeling that she hadn't slept very much the night before. There were dark rings under her eyes and although she'd put on lipstick, most of it had missed her lips. "This island is haunted!" she went on.

"What do you mean?" Eric asked.

"Last night ... my window ... it was horrible."

"I've got quite a nice window," Tim said.

"I mean ... I saw something! A human skull. It was dancing in the night air."

So she'd seen it too! I was about to chip in, but then Eric interrupted. "I don't think it's going to help, sharing our bad dreams," he said.

"I didn't dream it," Brenda insisted.

"We've got to do something!" Mark cut in. "First Rory, then Sylvie. At this rate, there won't be any of us left by lunch-time."

"I don't want any lunch," Libby muttered.

"We need to talk about this," Eric said. "We need to work something out. But there's no point starting until we're all here." He glanced at the clock. "Where the hell is Janet?"

"Maybe she's in the bath," Tim suggested.

"In the water or underneath it?" Eric growled.

The minute hand on the kitchen clock ticked forward. It was nine o'clock. Suddenly Mark stood up. "I'm going upstairs," he announced.

"You're going back to bed?" Tim asked.

"I'm going to find her."

He left the room. The rest of us followed him, tiptoeing up the stairs and along the corridor with a sense of dread. Actually, Eric didn't exactly tiptoe. He was so fat that it must have been quite a few years since his toes *had* tips. Mark Tyler had moved quickly, taking the stairs four at a time as if they were hurdles and he was back at the Olympic games at Atlanta. He was outside the door when we arrived.

"She's overslept," Tim said to me. "She's fine. She's just overslept."

Eric knocked on her door. There was no answer. He knocked again, then turned the handle. The door opened.

The hairdresser had overslept all right, but nothing was ever going to wake her up again. She had been stabbed during the night. She was lying on her back on a four-poster bed like the one in our room, only smaller. The bed was old. The paint had peeled off the posts and there was a tear in the canopy above her. In fact the whole room looked shabby, as if it had been missed out by the decorators. Maybe I noticed all this because I didn't want to look at the body. You may think I'm crazy, but dead people upset me. And when I did finally look at her, I got a shock.

Whoever had killed her hadn't used a knife. There was something sticking out of her chest and at first I thought it was some sort of rocket. It was silver, in the shape of a sort of long pyramid, with four legs jutting out. Then, slowly, it dawned on me what I was looking at. It was a model, a souvenir of the building that I had climbed up with Tim only the year before.

It was incredible. But true. Janet Rhodes had been stabbed with a model of the Eiffel Tower.

"The Eiffel Tower!" Tim muttered. His face was the colour of sour milk. "It's an outrage. I mean, it's meant to be a tourist attraction!"

"Why the Eiffel Tower?" I asked.

"Because it's famous, Nick. People like to visit it."

"No – I don't mean, why is it a tourist attraction. I mean, why use it as a murder weapon? It's certainly a strange choice. Maybe someone is trying to tell us something."

"Well, they certainly told Janet something," Tim said.

We were back at the breakfast table. The scrambled eggs were cold and congealed and looked even less appetizing than before. All the Frosties had gone soggy. But it didn't matter. There was no way anybody was going to eat anything today. The way things were going, I wondered if any of us would ever eat anything again.

Nobody was talking very much. I knew why. But it was Brenda who put it into words.

"Do you realize..." she began, and for once her voice was hoarse and empty. "Do you realize that the killer could be sitting here, at this table."

Tim looked around. "But there's only us here!"

"That's what she means, Tim," I said. "She's saying that the killer could be one of us!"

Brenda nodded. "I know it's one of us. One of us got up last night and went down the corridor." She shuddered. "I thought I heard squeaking last night…"

"That was Tim," I said. "He snores."

"No. It was a floorboard. Somebody left their room…"

"Did anyone else hear anything last night?" Eric asked.

There was a pause. Then Libby nodded. "I have the room next to Mark," she said. She turned to look at him. "I heard your door open just after midnight. I heard you go into the corridor."

"I went to the toilet," Mark replied. His dark face had suddenly got darker. He didn't like being accused.

"You went to the toilet in the corridor?" Tim asked.

"I went to the toilet which is across the corridor, opposite my room. I didn't go anywhere near Janet."

"What about the skull?" Brenda whispered. Eric scowled. He had forgotten about the dancing skull. "I know you say it's a dream, Eric," she went on. "But that's typical of you. You never believed anything I said, even when we were at school. Well, believe me now…" she took a deep breath. "Maybe it wasn't a ghost or a monster. Maybe it was someone in a mask. But they were there! I was awake. I jumped out of bed and went over to the window but by the time I got there, seconds later, they'd gone. Vanished into thin air..."

"It wasn't a dream," I said. "I saw it too."

"You?" Eric sneered at me.

I nodded.

"I didn't see anything," Tim said.

"You were asleep, Tim. But it was definitely there. It came out of nowhere ... like a magic trick. A rabbit out of a hat!"

"You saw a rabbit too?" Tim asked.

We all ignored him. "Any one of us could have climbed out onto the terrace," Brenda said. "Any one of us could have killed Janet. And Rory. And Sylvie! How do we know that she wasn't strangled or poisoned or something?"

"I think she *was* poisoned," I said.

Everyone looked at me so I told them about the sweet wrapper and Sylvie's love of chocolate. It was strange. Everyone in the room was ten years older than me but suddenly I was in control.

Not for long, though. Eric Draper, the ex-head boy, raised his hands. "Ladies and gentlemen," he announced. "I don't think we should jump to conclusions. Why would any of us sitting at this table want to kill Rory or Sylvie or Janet?"

"Mark used to go out with Sylvie," Libby said. She was staring at him. "When she broke up with you, you told me you wanted to kill her."

"That was ten years ago!" Mark protested. He jerked a finger at Libby. "Anyway, what about *you*? You nearly *did* kill Rory with that bicycle pump..."

"Yes. And what about you!" Tim pointed at Eric. "You say your name's Eric, so why are you wearing a dressing-gown that belongs to Ed?"

It took Eric a few seconds to work out what Tim was getting at. "Those are my initials, you idiot!" he snapped. He took a deep breath and raised his hands. "Look," he went on. "There's no point arguing amongst ourselves. We have to stick together. It could be our only hope."

The others fell silent. I had to admit, Eric was speaking sense. Blaming each other wouldn't help.

"Both Brenda and ... Tim's little brother saw somebody last night," he went on. I didn't know why he couldn't call me by my name. "Now that could have been one of us, dressing up to frighten the others. But remember, we were all inside the house ... and this thing, whatever it was, was outside. So maybe it was someone else. Maybe it was someone we don't know about."

"You mean ... someone hiding on the island?" Mark said.

"Exactly. We know we can't call the police. We know we're stuck here. But it seems to me that the first thing we have to do is find out if there's anyone else here."

"We've got to organize a search party," I said.

Tim shook his head. "This is no time for a party, Nick," he muttered.

"You're right, Eric," Libby said. "We've got to go over the island from head to tail."

"But at the same time, I think we should keep an eye on each other," Brenda said. "I'll feel safer that way."

Eric went upstairs to get changed. Mark went with him. From now on, we were going to do everything in pairs. Brenda and Libby cleared the breakfast things. I'd already noticed that most of the food in the house was in tins – which was just as well. Even the cleverest killer couldn't tamper with a tin, so at least we wouldn't starve. At half past nine we all met in the hall. Then we put on our coats and went outside.

The search began back at the jetty, right at the head of the crocodile. The idea was that we could cover the entire island, working like the police searching a wood when someone has gone missing. That is, we kept ten metres apart, always in sight of one another, moving across the island in a line. It was a beautiful day.

The sun was shining and the sea was blue, but even so I could feel a chill breeze on Crocodile Island. And there was something else. I couldn't escape the feeling that I was being watched. It was weird. Because it was obvious that there wasn't anybody in sight ... not even so much as a sheep or a cow.

It only took us an hour to cover the island. There really wasn't very much there. Most of it was covered in gorse that only came up to the knee, which no killer could have hidden behind – unless, of course, he happened to be extremely small. There were a few trees but we checked the branches and Tim even climbed one to see if anyone was hiding at the top. Then I climbed up to help Tim down again and we moved on. We came to a couple of ruined outbuildings. I went inside. There was nobody there – but I did see something. Another security camera, fixed to the brickwork. Of course, a rich man like Rory would have had to be careful about security. I remembered the camera I had noticed in the kitchen. He had probably covered the whole island. Was that why I had felt we were being watched?

We went past the house and continued towards the crocodile's tail. The ground rose steeply up, finally arriving at a narrow point at least twenty metres above the sea. This was what I had seen from the boat. Six great rocks, steel grey and needle-sharp, rose out of the water far below. Looking down made my head spin. I wondered briefly if there might be a cave somewhere, perhaps tucked underneath the lip where we were standing. But then a wave rolled in, crashing against the cliff face. If there was a killer down there, he'd be soaking wet. And anyway, as far as I could see, there was no way down.

We moved away, retracing our steps. There was nobody outside the house, but how about inside? Starting in the hall, we went from room to room: the library, the dining-room, the conservatory, the hall and so on. We looked behind curtains, under tables, in the fireplaces and up the chimneys. Tim even looked in the grandfather clocks. Maybe he thought he'd find somebody's grandfather. We covered the ground floor and then went up to the first. Here were the bedrooms, with our names still attached to the doors. We went into every one of them. There was nobody there ... apart from the three very dead bodies. It wasn't easy searching those particular rooms, but we made ourselves ... although I think Tim was wasting his time doing it with his eyes tightly shut.

Nobody in the rooms. Nobody in the corridors. We found the attic but all that was there was a water tank. Tim dipped his head in and I made a mental note not to drink any more water. Not with his dandruff. Eventually, we gave up. We had been everywhere. There was nowhere else to look.

We started to go back down to the kitchen but had only got halfway there when Libby let out a little gasp.

"What is it?" Eric demanded.

"There." She pointed at the wall at the end of the corridor. "I don't know why I didn't see it before!"

What she had seen was a black-and-white photograph in a silver frame. It was hanging right in the middle of the wall with enough space around it to make it stand out. The question was – had Rory hung it there? Or had it been someone else? Was this something we were meant to see?

The photograph showed nine teenagers, all of them wearing the same uniform. It's funny how people change in ten years – but I recognized them at once: Eric Draper, Janet Rhodes, Mark Tyler, Brenda Blake, Sylvie Binns, Libby Goldman, Rory McDougal and Tim. Tim looked the weirdest of them all. He'd had long hair then, and spots. Lots of spots. Of course, I wouldn't have looked too great myself when the picture had been taken – but then I would only have been four years old.

There was one face, however, that I didn't know. He was standing at the edge of the group, slightly apart; a thin, gangly teenager with curly hair and glasses. He was wearing an anorak and had the sort of face you'd expect to see on a train-spotter. "Who's he?" I asked.

"That's Johnny!" Brenda replied. "Johnny Nadler. He was one of my best friends…"

"And mine," Libby agreed. "Everyone liked Johnny. We used to hang out with him in the yard." She walked closer to the photograph. "I remember when this was taken. It was prize-giving day. He came second in geography. I came first."

"Wait a minute," I interrupted. "Everyone in this photograph is here on Crocodile Island. Everyone except Johnny Nadler!"

"You're right!" Mark agreed. "Why wasn't he invited?"

"Because he's the killer!" Eric snapped. "He's got to be!"

"But why would Johnny want to kill Rory?" Brenda asked. "The two of them were friends. And every day after school he used to catch the bus with Sylvie – even though it took him eight miles in the wrong direction. That's how much he liked her."

"He let Janet cut his hair," Libby went on. "She accidentally cut a chunk out of his ear, but he didn't mind. In fact he laughed all the way to the hospital. Johnny wouldn't hurt anyone."

"What else can you tell me about him?" I asked.

"He came second in history as well as geography," Eric said. "He was really clever."

"He was always playing with model planes and cars," Mark added. "He used to build them himself. We always said he'd be an inventor when he left school but in fact he ended up working at Boots. I saw him there once, when I went in to get some ointment." He blushed. "I had athlete's foot."

"Did any of the rest of you ever see him again?" I asked.

Everyone shook their heads. I looked at the photograph again. It did seem strange that he was the only one in the picture who hadn't been invited to Crocodile Island. But did that make him the killer? And if so, where on earth was he? We had searched the entire island and we were certain now that we were the only ones who were there.

Eric looked at his watch. It was half past twelve. "I suggest we continue this meeting downstairs," he said.

"I need to change," Brenda said.

"Me too," Libby agreed.

Everyone started to move in different directions.

"Hold on a minute!" I said. "I thought we were all going to stick together. I think we should all stay in this room."

"Don't be ridiculous!" Eric snapped. "We

have to eat something. It's lunch-time. And anyway, we've just searched the island. We know there's nobody else here."

"Well, I'm staying with Tim," I said.

"How do you know I'm not the killer?" Tim demanded.

Because whoever killed Rory and the others is brilliant and fiendish and you still have trouble tying your shoelaces. That was what I thought, but I didn't say anything. I just shrugged.

"I don't want to be near anyone," Libby said. "I feel safer on my own."

"Me too." Brenda nodded. "And I'm certainly not having anyone in the room with me while I'm changing."

"We can meet in ten minutes," Eric said. "We're inside the house. We know there's nobody else on the island. We'll meet in the dining-room at twenty to one."

He was wrong of course. This was one little group that was never going to meet again. But how could we know that? We were scared and we weren't thinking straight.

Tim and I went back to our room. Tim scratched his head, which was still damp from the water tank. "Johnny could be hiding on the island," he said. "What if there's a secret room?"

The same thought had already occurred to me, but I'd tapped every wall and every wooden panel and nothing had sounded hollow. "I don't think there are any secret rooms, Tim," I said.

"But you can't be sure…" Tim began to tap his way along the wall, his eyes half-closed, listening for a hollow sound. A few moments later, he straightened up, excited. "There's definitely something on the other side here!" he cried.

"I know, Tim," I said. "That's the window."

I left him in the bedroom, drying his hair, and went back downstairs. I was going to join the others in the dining-room. But I never got that far. I was about halfway down when I heard it. A short, sudden scream. Then a crashing sound. It had come from somewhere outside.

I ran down the rest of the way, through the hall and out the front door. Mark Tyler appeared, running round the side of the house.

"What was it…?" he demanded. He was trying not to sound scared but it wasn't working.

"Round the back?"

We went there together, moving more slowly now, knowing what we were going to find, not wanting to find it. The kitchen door opened and Brenda Blake came out. I noticed she was breathing heavily.

This time it was Libby Goldman. I'm afraid she had recorded her last episode of *Libby's Lounge* and for her the final credits were already rolling. Why had she gone outside? Maybe she'd decided to light up one of her cigarettes – in which case, this was one time when smoking certainly had been bad for her health. Fatal, in fact. But it hadn't been the tobacco that had killed her. Something had hit her hard on the head: something that had been dropped from above. I looked up, working out the angles. We were directly underneath the battlements. Behind them, the roof was flat. It would have been easy enough for someone to hide up there, to wait for any one of us to step outside. Libby must have come out to get a breath of fresh air before the meeting. Air wasn't something she'd be needing again.

There were footsteps on the gravel. Eric and Tim had arrived. They stared in silence. Mark stretched out a finger and pointed. It took me a minute to work out what he was pointing at. That was how much his finger was trembling.

And there it was, lying in the grass. At first I didn't recognize the object that had been dropped from the roof and which had fallen right onto Libby Goldman. I mean, I knew what it was – but I couldn't believe that that was what had been used.

It was a big round ball: a globe. The sort of thing you find in a library. Maybe it had been in Rory's library before the killer had carried it up to the roof. The United States of America was facing up. It was stained red.

I looked at Eric Draper. His mouth had

dropped open. He looked genuinely shocked. Mark Tyler was standing opposite him, staring. Brenda Blake was to one side. She was crying.

One of them had to be faking it. I was certain of it. One of them had to have climbed down from the room after watching Libby fall. There was nobody else here. One of them had to be the killer.

But which one?

MORE MURDER

Eric Draper? Brenda Blake? Or Mark Tyler?

It was early evening and Tim and I had gone for a walk – supposedly to clear our heads. But the truth was, I wanted to be alone with him and somehow I felt safer away from the house. It struck me that all the deaths had taken place inside or near the building. And if we stayed too close to the house something else might strike me – a falling piano or a model of the Taj Mahal, for example.

I glanced down at the piece of paper I was holding in my hand. I had made a few notes just before we left:

RORY McDOUGAL – Killed with a sword.
SYLVIE BINNS – Poisoned.
JANET RHODES – Stabbed with an Eiffel Tower!

LIBBY GOLDMAN – Knocked down with a globe.

There was a pattern in there somewhere but I just couldn't see it. Maybe some fresh air would help after all.

"I've got an idea!" Tim said.

"Go ahead, Tim," I said.

"Maybe I could swim back over to the coast and get some help."

We were sitting on the jetty. Today the sea was flat, the waves caught as if in a photograph. I could just make out the mainland, a vague ribbon lying on the horizon. The sun was setting fast. How many of us would see it rise again?

I shook my head. "No, Tim. It's too far."

"It can't be more than five miles."

"And you can't swim."

"Oh yes. I'd forgotten." He glanced at me. "But you can."

"I can't swim five miles!" I said. "The water's too cold. And there's too much of it. No. Our only hope is to solve this before the killer strikes again."

"You're right, Nick." Tim closed his eyes and sat in silence for a minute. Then he opened them again. "Maybe we could get one of the others to swim…"

"One of the others *is* the killer!" I said. "I saw someone out on the terrace, wearing a skeleton

135

mask. I don't know how they managed to disappear so quickly – but I wasn't imagining it. Brenda saw them too."

"Maybe it was Mark! He's a fast mover."

"And just now … when Libby Goldman was killed. Someone must have climbed up onto the roof." I thought back. "Brenda was out of breath when she came into the garden…"

"She could have been singing!"

"I doubt it. But she could have been running. She drops the globe, then runs all the way downstairs…"

A seagull flew overhead, crying mournfully. I knew how it felt. I almost wanted to cry myself.

"What's missing is the motive," I went on. "Think back, Tim. You were at school with these people. There are only three of them left – Brenda, Mark and Eric. Would any of them have any reason to kill the rest of you?"

Tim sighed. "The only people who ever threatened to kill me," he said, "were the teachers. My French teacher once threw a piece of chalk at me. And when that missed, he threw the blackboard."

"How did you get on with Mark Tyler?"

"We were friends. We used to play conkers together." He scratched his head. "I did once miss his conker and break three of his fingers, but I don't think he minded too much."

"How about Brenda Blake?"

Tim thought back. "She was in the school choir," he said. "She was also in the rugby team. She used to sing in the scrum." He scratched his head. "We used to tease her a bit but it was never serious."

"Maybe she didn't agree."

The waves rolled in towards us. I looked out at the mainland, hoping to catch sight of Horatio Randle and his boat, the *Silver Medal*. But the sea was empty, darkening as the sun dipped behind it. What had the old fisherman said when he'd dropped us? *"I'll be back in a couple of days."* It had been Wednesday when we arrived. He might not return until the weekend. How many passengers would there be left waiting for him?

"How about Eric Draper?" I asked.

"What about him?"

"He could be the killer. It would have to be someone strong to carry the globe up to the roof in the first place. Can you remember anything about him?"

Tim laughed. "He was a great sport. I'll never forget the last day of term when the seven of us pulled off his trousers and threw him in the canal!"

"What?" I exclaimed. "You pulled off his trousers and threw him in the canal? Why?"

"Well, he was the head boy. And he'd always been bossy. It was just a bit of fun. Except that he nearly drowned. And the canal was so polluted, he had to spend six months in hospital."

"Are you telling me that the seven of you nearly killed Eric?" I was almost screaming. "Hasn't it occurred to you that this whole thing could be his revenge?"

"But it was just a joke!"

"You almost killed him, Tim! Maybe he wasn't amused."

I stood up. It was time to go back to the house. The other three would be waiting for us ... if they'd managed to survive the last half-hour.

"I wish I'd never come here," Tim muttered.

"I wish you'd never come here," I agreed.

"Poor Libby. And Sylvie. And Janet. And Rory, of course. He was first."

We walked a few more steps in silence. Then I suddenly stopped. "What did you say, Tim?" I demanded.

"I didn't say anything!"

"Yes, you did! Before you weren't saying anything, you were saying something."

"I asked which side of the bed you wanted."

"No. That was yesterday." I played back what he had just said and that was when I saw it, the pattern I'd been looking for. "You're brilliant!" I said.

"Thanks!" Tim frowned. "What have I done?"

"Tell me," I said. "Did Libby come first in

anything at school? And was it ... by any chance ... geography?"

"Yes. She did. How did you know?"

"Let's get back inside," I said.

I found Eric, Mark and Brenda in the drawing-room. This was one of the most extraordinary rooms in the house – almost like a chapel with a great stained glass window at one end and a high, vaulted ceiling. Rory McDougal had obviously fancied himself as a musician. There was even a church organ against the wall, the silver pipes looming over us. Like so many of the other rooms, the walls were lined with old weapons. In here they were antique pistols; muskets and flintlocks. All in all, we couldn't have chosen a worse house to share with a mass murderer. There were more weapons than you'd find in the Tower of London and I just hoped that they weren't as real as they looked.

The three survivors were sitting in heavy, leather chairs. I stood in front of them with the organ on one side and a row of bookshelves on the other. Everyone was watching me and I felt a bit like Hercule Poirot at the end of one of his cases, explaining it to the suspects. The only trouble was, this wasn't the end of the case. I was still certain that I was talking to the murderer. He or she had to be one of the people in the room.

Somewhere outside, a clock chimed the hour. It was nine o'clock. Night had fallen.

"Seven of you were invited to Crocodile Island," I began. "And I see now that you all have something in common."

"We went to the same school," interrupted Tim.

"I know that, Tim. But there's something else. You all got prizes for coming first. You've already told me that Rory was first in maths. Libby was first in geography..."

"What's this got to do with anything?" Eric snapped.

"Don't you see? Libby was first in geography and someone dropped a globe on her head. Someone told me that Sylvie Binns came first in chemistry and we think she was poisoned."

"Janet came first in French..." Mark murmured.

"...which would explain why she was stabbed with a model of the Eiffel Tower. And Rory McDougal came first in maths."

"He was stabbed too," Eric said.

"He was more than stabbed. He was divided!"

There was a long silence.

"That's the reason why Johnny Nadler wasn't invited to the island," Brenda said. "He never came first in anything. He was second..."

"But that means..." Eric had gone pale. "I came first in history."

"I came first in sport," Mark said.

Brenda nodded. "And I came first in music."

We all turned to look at Tim. But he couldn't have come first in anything ... could he? I noticed he was blushing. He licked his lips and looked the other way.

"What did you come first in, Tim?" I asked.

"I didn't..." he began, but I could tell he was lying.

"We have to know," I said. "It could be important."

"I remember..." Brenda began.

"All right," Tim sighed. "I got first prize in needlework."

"Needlework!" I exclaimed.

"Well ... yes. It was a hobby of mine. Just for a bit. I mean..." He was going redder and redder. "I didn't even want the prize. I just got it. It was for a handkerchief..."

The idea of my sixteen-year-old brother winning a prize for an embroidered hanky made my head spin. But this wasn't the time to laugh. Hopefully I'd be able to do that later.

"Wait a minute! Wait a minute!" Eric said. He looked annoyed. Maybe it was because I was ten years younger than him and I was the one who'd worked it out. "I came first in history – and you're saying I'm going to be killed ... *historically?*"

"That's what it looks like," I said.

"But how…?"

I pointed at the wall, at the flintlock pistols on the wooden plaques. "Maybe someone will use one of those," I said. "Or there are swords, arrows, spears … that bear upstairs is even holding a blunderbuss. This place is full of old weapons."

"What about me?" Brenda whispered.

"You're not an old weapon!" Tim said.

"I came first in music." Brenda glared at the organ as if it was about to jump off the wall and eat her.

"But who's *doing* this?" Mark cut in. "I mean … it's got to be someone in this room. Right? We know there's nobody else on the island. There can't be anybody hiding. We've searched everywhere."

"It's him!" Brenda pointed at Eric. "He never forgave us for throwing him in the canal. This is his revenge!"

"What about *you?*" Eric returned. "You once said you were going to kill us all. It was in the school yard. I remember it clearly!"

"That's true!" Mark said.

"You used to bully me all the time," Brenda wailed. "Just because I had pigtails. And crooked teeth."

"And you were fat," Tim reminded her.

"But I didn't mean it, when I said that." She turned to Mark. "You said you were going to kill Tim when he broke all your fingers with that conker!"

"I only broke three of them!" Tim interrupted.

"I didn't much like Tim," Mark agreed. "And you're right. I would have quite happily strangled him. Not that it would have been easy with three broken fingers. But I never had any argument with you or with Eric or any of the others. Why would I want to kill you?"

"It's still got to be one of us," Eric insisted. He paused. "It can't be Tim," he went on.

"Why not?" Tim asked.

"Because this whole business is the work of a fiendish madman and you're not fiendish. You're just silly!"

"Oh thanks!" Tim looked away.

"I know it's not me…" Eric went on.

"That's what you say," Brenda sniffed.

"I know it's not me, so it's got to be Brenda or Mark."

"What about Sylvie?" Tim suggested.

"She's already dead, Tim," I reminded him, quietly.

"Oh yes."

"This is all irrelevant," Mark said. "The question is – what are we going to do? We could be stuck on this island for days, or even weeks. It all depends on when Captain Randle comes back. And by then it could be too late!"

"I'd like to make a suggestion," I said. Everyone stopped and looked at me. "The first thing is, we've all got to keep each other in sight."

"The kid's right," Mark agreed. "So long as we can see each other, we're going to be safe."

"That's true!" Tim exclaimed. "All we have to do is keep our eyes open and everything will be fine." He turned to me. "You're brilliant, Nick. For a moment there I was getting really worried."

Then all the lights went out.

It happened so suddenly that for a moment I thought it was just me. Had I been knocked out or somehow closed my eyes without noticing? The last thing I saw was the four of them – Eric, Brenda, Mark and Tim – sitting in their chairs as if caught in a photograph. Then everything was black. There was no moon that night and even if there had been the stained glass window would have kept most of the light out. Darkness came crashing onto us. It was total.

"Don't panic!" Eric said.

There was a gunshot. I saw it, a spark of red on the other side of the room.

Tim screamed and for a horrible moment I wondered if he had been shot. I forced myself to calm down. He'd come first in needlework. Nobody would be aiming a gun at him.

"Tim!" I called out.

"Can I panic now?" he called back.

"Eric…?" That was Mark's voice.

And then there was a sort of groaning sound, followed by a heavy thud. At the same time I heard a door open and close. I stood up, trying to see through the darkness. But it was hopeless. I couldn't even make out my own hand in front of my face.

"Tim?" I called again.

"Nick?" I was relieved to hear his voice.

"Eric?" I tried.

Silence.

"Brenda?"

Nothing.

"Mark?"

The lights came back on.

There were only two people alive in the room. I was standing in front of my chair. One more step and I'd have put my foot through the coffee table. Tim was *under* the coffee table. He must have crawled there when the lights went out. Eric was on the floor. He had been shot. There was a flintlock pistol, still smoking, lying on the carpet on the other side of the room. It must have been taken off the wall, fired and then dropped. At least, that's what it looked like. Brenda was sitting in her chair. She was dead too. One of the organ pipes – the largest – had been pulled down on top of her. That must have been the thud I had heard. Brenda had sung her last opera. The only music she needed now was a hymn.

There was no sign of Mark.

"Are you all right, Tim?" I demanded.

"Yes!" Tim sounded surprised. "I haven't been murdered!" he exclaimed.

"I noticed." I waited while he climbed out from underneath the coffee table. "At least we know who the killer is," I said.

"Do we?"

"It's got to be Mark," I said. "Mark Tyler..."

"I always knew it was him," Tim said. "Call it intuition. Call it experience. But I knew he was a killer even before he'd done any killing."

"I don't know, Tim," I said. It bothered me, because to be honest Mark was the last person I would have suspected. And yet, at the same time, I had to admit ... it would have taken a fast mover to push the globe off the roof and make it all the way downstairs in time and Mark was the fastest person on the island.

"Where do you think he went?" Tim asked.

"I don't know."

We left the room carefully. In fact, Tim made me leave it first. The fact was that – unless I'd got the whole thing wrong – it was just the three of us now on the island; Mark could be waiting for us anywhere. Or waiting for Tim, rather. He had no quarrel with me. And that made me think. Tim had come first in needlework. Following the pattern of the other deaths, that meant he would probably be killed with some sort of needle. But what would that mean? A sewing needle dipped in poison? A hypodermic syringe?

Tim must have had the same thought. He was looking everywhere, afraid to touch anything, afraid even to take another step. We went out into the hall. The fire had died down and was glowing red. The front door was open.

"Maybe he went outside," Tim said.

"What would be the point?" I asked.

Tim shuddered. "Don't talk about points," he said.

We went outside. And that was where we found Mark. He had come first in sport but now he had reached the finishing line. Somebody had been throwing the javelin and they'd thrown it at him. It had hit him in the chest. He was lying on the grass, doing a good impersonation of a sausage on a stick.

"It's … it's … it's…" Tim couldn't finish the sentence.

"Yeah," I said. "It's Mark." There were a few leaves scattered around his body. That puzzled me. The nearest trees were ten metres away. But this wasn't the time to play the detective. There were no more suspects. And only one more victim.

I looked at Tim.

Tim looked at me.

We were the only two left.

NEEDLES

Tim didn't sleep well that night. Although I hadn't said anything, not wanting to upset him, even he had managed to work out that he had to be the next on the killer's list. He also knew that his own murder would have something to do with needlework. So he was looking for needles everywhere.

By one o'clock in the morning we knew that there were no sewing needles in the room, no knitting needles and no pine needles. Even so, it took him an hour to get into bed and several more hours to get to sleep. Mind you, nobody would have found it easy getting to sleep dressed in a full suit of medieval armour, but that still hadn't stopped Tim putting it on.

"There could be a poisoned needle in the mattress," he said. "Or someone could try and inject me with a syringe."

Tim didn't snore that night; he clanked. Every

time he rolled over he sounded like twenty cans of beans in a washing machine. I just hoped he wasn't planning to take a bath in the suit of armour the following morning. That way he could end up rusting to death.

At four-thirty, he woke up screaming.

"What is it, Tim?" I asked.

"I had a bad dream, Nick," he said.

"Don't tell me. You saw a needle."

"No. I saw a haystack."

I didn't sleep well either. I got cramp and woke up in the morning with pins and needles. I didn't tell Tim, though. He'd have had a fit.

We had breakfast together in the kitchen. Neither of us ate very much. For a start, we were surrounded by dead bodies, which didn't make us feel exactly cheerful. But Tim was also terrified. I'd managed to persuade him to change out of the armour but now he was worrying about the food. Were there going to be needles in the cereal? A needle in the tea? In the end, I gave him a straw with a tissue sellotaped over the end. The tissue worked as a filter and he was able to suck up a little orange juice and a very softly-boiled egg.

I have to say that for once I was baffled. It was still like being in an Agatha Christie novel – only this time I couldn't flick through to the last page and see who did it without bothering to read the rest. Personally, I had always thought Eric had been the killer. He seemed to have the strongest motive – being half-drowned on the last day of school. It was funny really. All eight of the old boys and girls of St Egbert's had disliked each other. But someone, somewhere, had disliked them all even more. The whole thing had been planned right down to the last detail. And the last detail, unfortunately, was Tim.

But who? And why?

Tim sat miserably at his end of the table, hardly daring to move. Why had he had to come first in *needlework* of all things? How was I supposed to find the needle that was going to kill him? I knew now that the only hope for me was to solve this thing before the killer struck one last time. And a nasty thought had already occurred to me. Would the killer stop with Tim? I wasn't meant to be part of this. I had never gone to St Egbert's. But I was a witness to what had happened and maybe I had seen too much.

I went over what had happened last night. We had always assumed that there was nobody else on the island, but thinking it through I knew this couldn't be true. We had all been sitting down: Brenda in front of the organ, Eric opposite her, Mark nearest the door and Tim and me on the sofa. But none of us had been anywhere near the light switch, and someone had most certainly turned off the lights – not just in the drawing-room but throughout the entire house. Somewhere down in the basement, there would be a main fuse switch. But that led to another question. If the killer had been down in the basement, then how had he or she managed to appear in the room seconds later to shoot Eric and push the organ pipe onto Brenda?

At the time, I had assumed that Mark had committed the last two murders. There had been a shot, then a thud, then the opening and closing of a door. But a few seconds later, Mark had himself been killed. And what about the leaves that I had seen lying next to his body? How had they got there?

I thought back to the other murders. Rory first. We had all been on the island and we had all separated. Any one of us could have attacked him and, immediately afterwards, left the chocolate on the bed for Sylvie to find. That was the night I had seen the face at the window. A face that had appeared and disappeared – impossibly – in seconds. And then we had found Janet. I remembered her lying in her bed, stabbed by a model of the Eiffel Tower. Her room had been shabby. There had been a tear in the canopy ... I had remarked on it at the time. Why had it caught my eye?

Libby Goldman next. The television presenter had been knocked down with a model globe. There was something strange about that, too. Someone must have carried it up to the roof and dropped it on her when she came out of the front door. But now that I thought about it, I hadn't seen the globe in any of the rooms when we had been searching the house. And that could only mean one thing. It had been on the roof from the very start, waiting for her...

Maybe you know how it is when you've been given a particularly nasty piece of home-work – an impossible equation or a fiendish bit of physics or something. You stare at it and stare at it, but it's all just ink on paper and you're about to give up when you notice something and suddenly you realize it's not so difficult after all. Well, that was what was happening to me now.

I remembered the search party, slowly criss-crossing the island. We had seen security cam-eras everywhere and from the day I had arrived, I had felt that I was being watched. There was a security camera in the kitchen. I looked up. It was watching me even now. Were there cameras in other rooms, too?

At the same time, I remembered something Mark had said, when we had found the old pho-tograph of St Egbert's. And in that second, as quickly as that, I suddenly knew everything.

"I've got it, Tim!" I said.

"So have I, Nick!" Tim cried.

I'd been so wrapped up in my own thoughts,

that I hadn't noticed Tim had been thinking too. Now he was staring at me with the sort of look you see on a fish when it's spent too long out of water.

"You know who did it?" I asked.

"Yes."

"Go on!"

"It's simple!" Tim explained. "First there were eight of us on the island, then seven, then six, then five..."

"I know," I interrupted. "I can count backwards."

"Well, now there are only two of us left. I know it wasn't me who committed the murders." He reached forward and snatched up a spoon. Then he realized what he'd done, put it down and snatched up a knife. He waved it at me. "So the killer must be you!" he exclaimed.

"What?" I couldn't believe what I was hearing.

"There's only us left. You and me. I know it wasn't me so it must have been you."

"But why would I want to kill everyone?" I demanded.

"You tell me!"

"I wouldn't! And I didn't! Don't be ridiculous, Tim."

I stood up. That was a mistake.

"Don't come near me!" Tim yelled, and suddenly he sprang out of his chair and jumped out of the window. This was an impressive feat. The window wasn't even open.

I couldn't believe what had happened. I knew Tim was stupid but this was remarkable even by his standards. Maybe sleeping in a suit of armour had done something to that tiny organism he called his brain. At the same time, I was suddenly worried. I knew who the killer was now and I knew who was lined up to be the next victim. Tim was outside the house, on his own. He had made himself into a perfect target.

I had no choice. I went after him, jumping through the shattered window. I could see Tim a short distance away, running towards the tail of Crocodile Island. I had no idea where he was going. But nor of course did he. He was panicking – just trying to put as much distance between the two of us as he could. Not easy considering he was trapped on a small island.

"Tim!" I called.

He didn't stop. I ran after him, following the path as it began to climb steeply up towards the cliffs. This was where the island tapered to a point. I slowed down. Tim had already reached the far end. He had nowhere else to go.

The wind blew his hair around his head as he turned to face me. He was still holding the knife. I noticed now that it was a butter knife. If he stabbed me with all his strength he might just manage to give me a small bruise. His face was pale and his eyes were wide open and staring. The last time I had seen him like this was when they had shown *Jurassic Park* on TV.

"Get back, Nick!" he yelled. It was hard to hear him above the crash of the waves.

"You're crazy, Tim!" I called back. "Why would I want to hurt you? I'm your brother. Think about all the adventures we've had together! I've saved your life lots of times." I thought of telling him that I loved him but he'd have known that wasn't true. "I quite like you!" I said. "You've looked after me ever since Mum and Dad emigrated to Australia. We've had fun together!"

Tim hesitated. I could see the doubt in his eyes. He lowered the butter knife. A huge wave rolled in and crashed against the rocks, spraying us both with freezing, salt water. I looked past Tim at the rocks, an idea forming in my mind. There were six iron grey rocks, jutting out of the sea. I had noticed them the day we had searched the island. And of course, rocks like that have a name. Long and slender with pointed tops, standing upright in the water…

They're called needles.

I'm not exactly sure what happened next but I do know that it all happened at the same time.

There was a soft explosion, just where Tim was standing. The earth underneath his feet seemed to separate, falling away.

Tim screamed and his arm jerked. The butter knife spun in the air, the sun glinting off the blade.

I yelled out and threw myself forward. Somehow my hands managed to grab hold of Tim's shirt.

"Don't kill me!" Tim whimpered.

"I'm not killing you, you idiot!" I yelled. "I'm saving you!"

We rolled back together, away from the edge of the cliff … an edge that was now several centimetres closer to us than it had been seconds before. I was dazed and there was grass in my mouth, but I realized that the killer had struck again. There had been a small explosive charge buried in the ground at the end of the cliff. Someone had detonated it and if I hadn't managed to grab hold of Tim, he would have fallen down towards to the sea, only to crash onto the needles fifty metres below.

We lay on the grass, panting. The sun was beating down on us. It was difficult to see. But then I became aware of a shadow moving towards us. I rolled over and looked up at the figure, limping towards us, a radio transmitter in one hand and a gun in the other.

"Well, well, well," he said. "It looks as if my little plan has finally come unstuck. And just when everything was going so well, too!"

Tim stared at the man. At his single eye, his

single leg, his huge beard. "It's … it's…" he began.

"It's Horatio Randle," I said. "Captain of the *Silver Medal,* the boat that brought us here."

"You got it in one, young lad!" he said.

"But that's not his real name," I went on. "Randle is an anagram. If you switch around the letters, you get…"

"Endral!" Tim exclaimed.

"Nadler," I said. "I think this must be Johnny Nadler. Your old school friend from St Egbert's."

The captain put down the radio transmitter. He had used it, of course, to set off the explosive charge a few moments before. He didn't let go of the gun. With his free hand, he reached up and pulled off the fake beard, the wig and the eye patch. At the same time, he twisted round and released the leg that he'd had tied up behind his back. It only took a few seconds but at once I recognized the thin-faced teenager I had seen in the photograph.

"It seems you've worked it all out," he muttered. His accent had changed too. He was no longer the jolly captain. He was a killer. And he was mad.

"Yes," I said.

"But it's impossible!" Tim burbled. "He couldn't have killed all the others. We looked! There was nobody else on the island!"

"It was Nadler all along," I said. I glanced

at him. The wind raced past and the waves crashed down.

He smiled. "Do go on," he snarled.

"I know what you did," I said. "Last Wednesday, you met us all at the quay, disguised as a captain. You'd sent everyone invitations to this reunion on the island and you even offered to pay a thousand pounds to make sure that they'd all come. Rory McDougal had nothing to do with it, of course. You'd killed him before we even set sail."

"That's right," Nadler said. He was smiling now. There was something horrible about that smile. He was sure this was one story I wouldn't be telling anyone else.

"You killed Rory and you left the poisoned chocolate for Sylvie. Then you dropped us on the island and sailed away again. There was no need for you to stay. Everything was already prepared."

"Are you saying … he wasn't here when he killed everyone?" Tim asked. He was still lying on the grass. There was a buttercup lodged behind his ear.

"That's right. Don't you remember what Mark told us when we were looking at the picture? He said that Johnny Nadler wanted to be an inventor when he left school. He said he was always playing with planes and cars." I glanced at the transmitter lying on the ground just a few feet away. "I assume they were radio-controlled planes and cars," I said.

"That's right!" Tim said. "He was brilliant, Nick! He once landed a helicopter on the science teacher's head!"

"Well, that's how he killed everyone on the island – after he'd finished with Rory McDougal and Sylvie Binns." I took a deep breath, wondering if there was anything I could do. Tim was right next to the edge of the cliff. I was a couple of metres in front of him. We were both lying down. Nadler was standing over us, aiming with the gun. If we so much as moved, he could shoot us both. I had to keep talking and hope that I might somehow find a way to distract him.

"Janet Rhodes was stabbed with an Eiffel Tower," I went on. "But I noticed that there was a tear in the canopy above her bed. I should have put two and two together and realized that the Eiffel Tower was always there, above the bed. It must have been mounted on some sort of spring mechanism. Nadler knew that was where she'd be sleeping. All he had to do was press a button and send the model plunging down. He was probably miles away when he killed her."

"That's right!" Nadler giggled. "I was back on the mainland. I was nowhere near!"

"But what about the face you saw?" Tim asked. "The skull at the window! Brenda saw it too!"

"You've already answered that one, Tim," I said. "A remote control helicopter or something with a mask hanging underneath. Nadler controlled that too. It was easy!"

"But how could he see us?"

I glanced at Nadler and he nodded. He was happy for me to explain how it had been done.

"The whole island is covered in cameras," I said. "That was Rory's security system. We've been watched from the moment we arrived. Nadler knew where we were every minute of the day."

"Right again!" Nadler grinned. He was pleased with himself, I could see that. "It was easy to hack into McDougal's security system and redirect the pictures to my own TV monitor. I was even able to watch you in the bath!"

"That's outrageous!" Tim was blushing. He knew that Nadler would have seen him playing with his plastic duck.

"Nadler had positioned the globe up on the roof," I went on. "If we'd gone up and looked we'd probably have found some sort of ramp with a simple switch. He waited until Libby Goldman came out of the front door and then he pressed the button that released the globe. It rolled forward and that was that. She never had a chance. He killed Eric and Brenda the same way. First he turned out the lights. Then he fired a bullet and brought down an organ pipe ...

160

both by remote control." I paused. "How about Mark Tyler?" I asked.

"The javelin was hidden in the branches of a tree," Nadler explained. "It was on a giant elastic band. Remote control again. It was just like a crossbow." He giggled for a second time. "Only bigger."

Well that explained the leaves. Some of them must have travelled with the javelin when it was fired.

"And that just left you, Tim," I said. "Nadler had to wait until you came out here. Then he was going to blow the ground out from beneath your feet and watch you fall onto the needles below. And with you dead, his revenge would be complete."

"Revenge?" Tim was genuinely puzzled. "But why did he want revenge? We never did anything to him!"

"I think it was because he came second," I said. I turned to Nadler. "You came second in every subject at school. And the boat you picked us up in. It was called the *Silver Medal*. I guess you chose the name on purpose. Because that's what you're given when you come second."

"That's right." Nadler nodded and now his face had darkened and his lips were twisted into an expression of pain. His finger tightened on the trigger and he looked at me with hatred in his eyes. "I came second in maths, second in chemistry, second in French, second in geography, second in history, second in music and second in sport. I even came second in needlework, even though my embroidered tea towel was much more beautiful than your brother's stupid handkerchief!"

"It was a lovely handkerchief!" Tim said.

"Shut up!" Nadler screamed and for a moment I was afraid he was going to shoot Tim then and there. "Do you have any idea how horrible it is coming second?" he went on. Saliva flecked at his lips. The hand with the gun never moved. "Coming last doesn't matter. Coming fifth or sixth ... who cares? But when you come second, everyone knows. You've just missed! You've missed getting the prize by just a few marks. And everyone feels sorry for you. Poor old Johnny! He couldn't quite make it. He wasn't quite good enough."

He took a deep breath. "I've been coming second all my life. I go for jobs and I get down to the last two in the interviews but it's always the other person who gets it. I went out with a girl but then she decided to marry someone else because as far as she was concerned, I was Number Two. When I've tried to sell my inventions, I've discovered that someone else has always got there first. Number Two! Number Two! Number Two! I hate being Number Two...!

"And it's all your fault!" He pointed the gun at Tim and now the fury was back in his eyes. "It all started at St Egbert's! That hateful school! That was where I started coming second and that was why I decided to have my revenge. You all thought you were clever beating me at everything. Well, I've showed you! I've killed the whole lot of you and I've done it in exactly the way you deserve!"

"You haven't killed me!" Tim exclaimed.

I didn't think it was a good idea to point this out. Nadler steadied the gun. "I'm going to do that now," he said. "Your body will still end up smashing into the needles so everything will have worked out the way it was meant to." He nodded at me. "I'll have to kill you too, of course," he continued. "You weren't meant to be here, but I don't mind. You sound too clever for your own good. I'm going to enjoy killing you too!"

He took aim.

"No!" I shouted.

He fired at Tim.

"Missed!" Tim laughed and rolled to one side. He was still laughing when he rolled over the side of the cliff.

"Tim!" I yelled.

"Now it's your turn," Nadler said.

I closed my eyes. There was nothing I could do.

There was a long pause. I opened them again. Nadler was still standing, but even as I watched he crumpled to the ground. Eric Draper, the fat solicitor, was standing behind him. There was blood all over his shirt and he was deathly pale. But he was still alive. He was holding the blunderbuss, which he must have taken from the bear. He hadn't fired it. He had used it like a club and knocked Nadler out.

"He only wounded me..." he gasped. "I woke up this morning. I came to find you..."

But I wasn't interested in Eric Draper, even if he had just saved my life. I crawled over to the cliff edge and looked down, expecting to see Tim, smashed to pieces, on the rocks below.

"Hello, Nick!" Tim said.

There was a gorse bush growing out of the side of the cliff. He had fallen right onto it. I held out a hand. Tim took it. I pulled him to safety and we both lay there in the sun, exhausted, glad to be alive.

We found the *Silver Medal* moored at the jetty and I steered it back towards the mainland. Eric was slumped on the deck. Johnny Nadler was down below, tied up with so much rope that only his head was showing. We weren't taking any chances after what had happened. We had already radioed ahead to the police. They would be waiting when we got to the mainland. Tim was standing next to me. We had left six dead bodies behind us on Crocodile Island. Well, I warned you that it was going to be a horror story.

"I'm sorry I thought you were the killer," Tim said. He was looking even more sheepish than ... well, a sheep.

"It's all right, Tim," I said. "It's a mistake anyone could have made." He swayed on his feet and suddenly I felt sorry for him. "Do you want to sit down?" I asked. "It's going to take us a while to get back."

Tim shook his head. "No." He blushed. "I can't!"

"Why not?"

"That bush I fell into. It was very prickly. My bottom's full of..."

"What?"

"...needles!"

I pushed down on the throttle and the boat surged forward. Behind us, Crocodile Island shimmered in the morning mist until at last it had disappeared.

MORE BOOKS BY ANTHONY HOROWITZ...

ANTHONY HOROWITZ

THE Power OF FIVE

FIVE ORDINARY TEENAGERS.

FIVE EXTRAORDINARY POWERS.

ONE CHANCE TO SAVE MANKIND.

OBLIVION

THE FINAL THRILLING EPISODE NOW UNLEASHED

FIND OUT HOW IT ALL BEGAN...
WWW.POWEROF5.CO.UK

GO BACK TO THE BEGINNING, AND DISCOVER WHERE IT ALL STARTED...

Raven's Gate
He always knew he was different.
First there were the dreams.
Then the deaths began.

Evil Star
It began with Raven's Gate.
But it's not over yet.
Once again the enemy is stirring.

Nightrise
Darkness covers the earth.
The Old Ones have returned.
The battle must begin.

Necropolis
An ancient evil is unleashed.
Five have the power to defeat it.
But one of them has been taken.

The first four volumes in the bestselling supernatural series by ANTHONY HOROWITZ

THE POWER OF FIVE
www.powerof5.co.uk

Meet Tim Diamond, the world's worst private detective, and his quick-thinking wisecracking younger brother Nick!

"His first job was to find some rich lady's pedigree Siamese cat. He managed to run it over on the way to see her. The second job was a divorce case – which you may think is run-of-the-mill until I tell you that the clients were perfectly happily married until he came along... There hadn't been a third case."

Collect all 4 hilarious Diamond Brothers investigations!

THE ALEX RIDER SERIES

Alex Rider – you're never
too young to die…

High in the Alps, death
waits for Alex Rider…

Sharks. Assassins. Nuclear
bombs. Alex Rider's in
deep water.

Alex Rider has 90 minutes
to save the world.

Once stung, twice as
deadly. Alex Rider wants
revenge.

He's back – and this time
there are no limits.

BOOKs rock!

Want to read more?

VISIT your local bookshop

- Get great recommendations for books you'll love
- Meet your favourite authors & illustrators at brilliant events
- Discover books you never knew existed!

 FIND YOUR LOCAL BOOKSHOP www.booksellers.org.uk/bookshopsearch

JOIN your local library

You can browse and borrow from a huge selection of books and get recommendations of what to read next from expert librarians – all for FREE!

You can also discover libraries' wonderful children's and family reading activities – such as reading groups (*see* www.chatterbooks.org.uk), author events and challenges (*see* www.summerreadingchallenge.org.uk).

Get Online

Explore www.worldbookday.com to discover a world of bonkersly brilliant beautiful books!

- Downloads and activities for your favourite books and authors
- Cool games, trailers and videos
- Fantastic competitions
- Author events in your area
- Sign up for the **FREE** monthly e-newsletter

And much, much more...

ANTHONY HOROWITZ is one of the most popular contemporary children's writers. Both The Power of Five and Alex Rider are number one bestselling series enjoyed by millions of readers worldwide.

When Anthony launched the Alex Rider series he created a phenomenon in children's books, spurring a new trend of junior spy books and inspiring thousands of previously reluctant readers. Hailed as a reading hero, Anthony has also won many major awards, including the Bookseller Association/Nielsen Author of the Year Award, the Children's Book of the Year Award at the British Book Awards, and the Red House Children's Book Award. The first Alex Rider adventure, *Stormbreaker*, was made into a blockbuster movie in 2006.

Anthony's other titles for Walker Books include the Diamond Brothers mysteries; *Groosham Grange* and its sequel, *Return to Groosham Grange*; *The Devil and His Boy*; *Granny*; *The Switch*; and a collection of horror stories, *More Bloody Horowitz*. Anthony also writes extensively for TV, with programmes including *Foyle's War*, *Midsomer Murders*, *Collision* and, most recently, *Injustice*. His latest novel, *The House of Silk*, is a brand new Sherlock Holmes adventure, written with the endorsement of the Conan Doyle Estate.

Although abandoned by both his sons, Anthony Horowitz continues to live in Clerkenwell with his wife, Jill Green, and the ghost of his dog, Lucky. You can find out more about Anthony and his books at:

www.anthonyhorowitz.com

www.alexrider.com

www.powerof5.co.uk